THE ROAD UPSTATE

A Junius Thompson Adventure

Dan Ackerman

Supposed Crimes LLC • Matthews, North Carolina

All Rights Reserved
Copyright © 2019 Dan Ackerman

Published in the United States.

ISBN: 978-1-944591-60-1

www.supposedcrimes.com

This book is typeset in Goudy Old Style.

For David

MARCH 5, 1954.

It had taken a lot of coaxing to get James Kelly to come out tonight, but it always did these days. Not that it had ever been easy to get him anywhere, but June had assumed that making the change from sleeping on the couch to sharing the bed would have loosened him up a little.

If anything, it had made things worse and June didn't know what to do with that.

Wait, probably.

June planted his elbow on the bar and leaned forward, resting his chin on his hand. James Kelly hadn't spoken to him for a solid ten minutes, but June was content to do nothing more than look at him for now.

He had a good profile – strong jaw, slightly aquiline nose, high cheekbones. In profile, he looked sterner than he did straight on. When viewed directly, James Kelly's features softened; he looked shy and almost pretty, instead of cold and handsome.

His rich brown skin glowed in the low light of the bar and June wanted to bury his face in the vampire's neck, loosen his tie and undo his buttons so he could leave kisses all over his throat. He should have been a movie star, June thought idly, or carved in marble.

"Stop looking at me like that," James Kelly warned.

June raised an eyebrow and glanced around the bar, wondering if James Kelly had picked up on something he hadn't. The place had long been one of June's favorite haunts. It welcomed unnatural creatures as well as those who searched for partners outside of the one man-one woman dynamic. "Looking at you like what?"

James Kelly's mouth twisted and June thought that he had about the handsomest scowl in the world.

"Like you're my boyfriend?"

The vampire tensed up at the very word. June hadn't had an occasion to use that term yet and James Kelly took it better than June had figured he would. He didn't walk out or tell June off, he just sat there, stiff and scowling.

"You know everyone here is queer, too, don't you?"

James Kelly shrugged.

"We're safe here."

"Until there's a vice raid," he pointed out.

June sighed, not irritated with James Kelly but with himself. He wasn't good at this, at hiding and keeping secrets. James Kelly, however, had learned to do it and did it well. He knew which dangers lurked where. Vice raids at bars and queer bashers in the alleys; racists waiting in white neighborhoods and anti-Semites who came out at night to graffiti kosher delis.

June lit a cigarette and offered one to James Kelly, who accepted.

They smoked in silence.

June ground out the butt in the ashtray. "I'm going on a trip in a week."

That got James Kelly's attention well enough. "Where?"

"Upstate. I've got some business to take care of."

The vampire frowned. "What kind of business?"

"Oh, no, nothing to worry about. Fertility rights and things like that, you know. Visit the orchards and the dairy farms."

"Oh. Alright."

"I'm sure you'll be glad to have me out of your hair for a while."

James Kelly graced him with an unkind look, his bourbon eyes narrowed. June had expected as much.

"No one dragging you out to bars full of fags or trying to get you to call your parents."

"Shut up."

June was quiet for no more than ten seconds. "Or."

James Kelly stayed frosty for a moment, then took the bait and asked, "Or what?"

"Or you could come with me."

The chill disappeared, a smile lighting up the other man's face. "It would be something, I bet!" Then the smile slid right off his face.

Before James Kelly could think of something that would go wrong, June clasped his hand. "Don't even go there, it would be fun. And I want you to come with me, I do."

"People will give us a hard time."

June shook his head. "Most of the people we're going to see, they all know me for what I am, whatever it is that we're calling it these days."

"And no one between here and Buffalo will—"

"Who said anything about Buffalo!" June interrupted.

James Kelly sighed. "You know what I meant."

"People won't know anything. We'll be just like, uh, Laurel and Hardy. Or, you know...Bing Crosby and Bob Hope. *Road to Singapore* or *Rio* or *Morocco* or wherever you want to go. I'll spring for matching outfits. I bet we have enough time to learn a few songs and dances."

The vampire rolled his eyes.

"You're killing me, kid. What's a guy gotta do to make you laugh these days?"

"I'm sorry."

He did sound genuinely reticent for his mood. June imagined that it had to be exhausting to live life the way he did, so he offered, "Let's say we call it a night, huh?"

James Kelly nodded, looking like he'd been offered an undeserved kindness, and left without another word. June fished out a few bills and tossed them on the bar, then made his rounds to say goodbye. He'd hoped to stay out a little longer, introduce James Kelly to a few friends to let them all know that he hadn't been making things up.

They'd all heard about him mooning over some Brooklyn vampire, they'd heard a lot of things about the two of them kissing at Peggy's party, but all the friends he ran into didn't seem to believe that there was anything to it. Even tonight, as he said goodbye and people asked if they were ever going to meet his boyfriend, they didn't seem to understand that the morose fellow at the bar had been his boyfriend.

June caught up with James Kelly outside, smoking on the street corner. "You come here often?" he asked.

James Kelly gave him a look and set off towards home.

June gave him his space until they got back to their building. Once they passed the threshold of their apartment, James Kelly relaxed.

He didn't leap into June's arms or anything like that, but shucked off his jacket and hung it up without huffing or scowling.

June skimmed a hand over James Kelly's back on his way into the living room. "So what do you think, though? Do you want to come along?"

James Kelly took a few steps further into the apartment, his arms crossed. "I don't know. Aren't you worried?"

"No."

"I should be so lucky," James Kelly scoffed.

June grinned at him.

"What?"

"Nothing. I like you is all." June put his arms around him. "Come with me."

"I don't know, June. I'm sorry."

"What about giving me a kiss?"

James Kelly leaned in but June stepped back, putting his hands on his shoulders. "Wait! Shouldn't we lock the doors? Draw the shades! God knows what would happen...! What if the neighbors saw!"

"Don't be mean," James Kelly scolded.

June rushed around, locking the doors and windows, then seizing James Kelly by the hand and pulling him towards their bedroom. He clasped him close. They could have been in *Anna Karenina*. "Do you think we'll be safe here?" he whispered conspiratorially.

James Kelly smiled. Out in the real world, he would have shrugged off June's embrace, he would have grown irritated with the teasing, but in the sanctuary of their apartment, he was real and warm. "Next time you should just go without me."

"What's the point in that? I want to go out *with* you. I want you to meet the people I know. No one believes we're together. I don't even think Peggy really believes me."

James Kelly pulled back. "Why should she? You haven't got a boyfriend, you've got, I don't know, a case of bedbugs that doesn't pay rent."

"Oh, don't be like that. I like the way you bite."

"And do you like the way I don't pay rent?"

"I do."

James Kelly crossed his arms.

"What, am I going to send you out to make a couple bucks breaking your back or sweeping floors?" June cradled James Kelly's check in his palm. "You're too good for that."

He wrinkled his nose. "I'm not better than—"

"No, you're not. You're *all* too good for how the world treats you." June put his other hand up and held his face in both hands. "I want...I want to take care of you. Is that terrible of me?"

"I don't need to be taken care of." James Kelly put his hands over June's and moved them away from his face.

"No, of course you don't, and I don't *need* to have a cat...no, don't, alright that was a bad analogy," June trailed off, doubting that the other man would take kindly to being compared to the cat.

Instead, he twined his fingers with June's. "But you like the way I come sit on your lap while you're reading?"

"I do like that. I also like the way you sit in the sink and watch me use the bathroom." He leaned in and kissed him. "I want to give you good things. I want you to let me."

"You give me everything."

June did not point out that there were a lot of things he couldn't give him. A sense of security or confidence in public, children—if he even wanted them, a wedding where his parents could feel proud and content at how well he had done for himself, and a thousand other things. They were all outside of what June could provide. He kissed him again and asked, "Bedtime?"

James Kelly nodded. "Bedtime," he agreed.

They crawled into bed together but didn't actually go to sleep. James Kelly stretched out on his stomach and June lightly ran his claws up and down his back.

June mused, "I've been thinking about getting a television."

"You've been thinking about getting a television for years at this point."

"Maybe someday I'll do it."

The vampire wiggled and stretched, arching up against June's claws. He sighed delectably when June scratched a little harder. "What would we even do?"

"With a television? I think the idea is to watch it."

James Kelly rolled over and gave June a fond push. "If we go upstate!"

"Three dairy farms, two apple orchards, a town called Lily Dale, and fertility festival in the Adirondacks."

"That's it?"

June sat up a little bit. "What do you mean that's it?"

"Only seven places want your help?"

"No, only six places want my help. I'm bringing a friend to Lily Dale, so that's a personal obligation, not a fertility job."

"Oh."

"But Lily Dale's the first stop!" June insisted, hoping it wouldn't take so little to dissuade James Kelly. "Lily Dale and this apple orchard, dairy farm, dairy farm, apple orchard, Adirondacks, dairy farm. Then back to Manhattan."

James Kelly nodded and settled on his side, his arm beneath his head. He put his other hand on June's waist. He didn't say anything else but fixed dreamy, half-closed eyes on June. He scooted a little closer; their bodies were not yet touching and June didn't particularly care if they did.

It wasn't what June was used to but there was something reassuring about the unhurried moments like these. It made him feel like he had forever.

June leaned in and kissed him, their bodies still separated but their hands finding a home on each other's skin.

James Kelly pulled back with a sigh.

June wondered if this would be one of those times where he

became overwhelmed with the reality of the situation. Sometimes the vampire carried on kissing and petting with enthusiasm, as much as June figured he'd had for any girl, but other times he seemed to struggle with what he wanted.

"I think about it too much," James Kelly always said at times like that.

This time, he ran his fingers over the small, pale gray horns that spiraled away from June's forehead, ran his fingers through June's hair and told him, "I'll never be a good boyfriend."

"Hmm?"

"All this going out and meeting friends and...and you know, *telling* anyone about any of this. It's." His face scrunched as he thought, searching for the right words. "It's not that I don't want to. I can't."

"Not yet, no," June agreed.

The other man didn't seem to know what to make of that.

"I didn't exactly figure that you could go from nothing to everything in two months. Plenty of folks spend their whole lives not telling a single soul. But we have years and years and I don't mind waiting as long as you don't mind me giving you a friendly nudge in the right direction now and again."

In a small, unsure voice, James Kelly asked, "Is it the right direction?"

"Do you mean about being with men or do you mean being open about it?"

"Both."

"Well, I've been doing it wrong for centuries at this point if it is," June joked. "But, you know, I was *made* by God to be how I am. I don't think the...what is it now? Homosexual, right?"

James Kelly nodded.

June didn't like the clinical taste of the term. "That part wasn't an accident. He doesn't make accidents."

The vampire let out a big sigh and closed the gap between them, put his arms around June and rested his forehead against June's chest. "I try."

"I know."

"You should be with someone else."

"I've *been* with someone else..." June told him then realized he'd misspoken, "I mean, I've been with other people before not that I've been seeing anyone else now. And I don't want to! I want to be with you."

James Kelly groaned.

"I can tell you all about why if you want. How do I love thee? Let me count the ways..."

"Don't."

"No?"

"No." He nestled closer. "I don't want to talk anymore. I don't want to think. I just...I just want to be with you."

June leaned in and kissed the top of his head. "I can do that."

MARCH 9, 1954.

The phone rang for about a minute straight before June remembered that James Kelly had gone out to feed. He tried not to think about it, not because the idea of the vampire feeding upset him on a moral level or turned his stomach, but because he was envious. James Kelly had taken blood from him once and June had sort of liked it. He thought that, with practice, it could be something as enjoyable for him as it was for the vampire. He just didn't know how to get James Kelly to bite him.

The ringing of the phone started to irritate him. He recalled that he was home alone and rushed to answer it.

"Hi!"

"Hello. June?"

"Elizabeth!" he cried and started chattering the way he did whenever he ended up talking to James Kelly's parents. "Hi, hello. Haven't seen you in a while! Ought to do something about that, don't you think? Anyway. How are you? How's Harold?"

Stilted but perfectly polite, she answered, "We're fine, thank you. How are you?"

"Good. Good. Getting ready for a trip."

The line was quiet for a second too long.

"Is, um, is my son there?"

Glad she couldn't see him squirming, he replied, "No, sorry, he's gone out. He should be home soon."

"I see."

"I'm awfully sorry. I really do tell him that you've been calling."

"Well. You know. His father and I are worried about him."

June settled onto the couch. "I'm taking very good care of him, I promise," he told her then realized that it probably wasn't what she wanted to hear about her only son. Or what she would have wanted to hear about any of her sons if she'd had more than just the one.

Harold and Elizabeth Rosenburg had sat down to eat with their son and the blue-skinned, horned stranger he'd brought over without screaming or saying anything horrible, but James Kelly had hardly talked to them since. June didn't know if something had transpired between them privately or if James Kelly simply couldn't face his parents afterward.

"Has he said anything to you?" Elizabeth asked.

"No. Has he said anything to you? Or...uh, well, did you say anything to him, maybe? You know he can be a bit prickly."

"I don't know." She went quiet for a bit. "I mean. I *asked*."

"Ah."

Defensive, she continued, "Who wouldn't ask! You've got a son that goes around with girls his whole life and he...well, he comes back from the war seven years *after* it ended, after we'd gotten a letter saying he'd *died* and now he's saying these things about being a...a vampire and now there's you..." Her voice warbled and he expected that she had tears in her eyes. "Oh, listen to me go. I don't know, June, I really don't."

"I can bother him about it if you want."

"No, no. Just. Tell him to call me. Please." She sniffled.

"I will. At least a dozen times."

"Thank you."

June didn't know what to say. "You're welcome," felt wrong and apologizing felt awkward, too. "Maybe you could call back in a little bit. About an hour."

"Alright, then. I'll give it a try. Goodbye." He was glad to hear that her voice had evened out again.

"Goodbye, Elizabeth."

He returned the phone to the receiver and stared at it for a while. Gordon walked across the back of the couch and butted his head against June's hand. June scratched the cat behind the ears and couldn't shake the feeling that he was ruining James Kelly's life, pulling him into some dark corner of society that the other man had opted out of altogether before meeting June. James Kelly had that choice, in a manner of speaking. Unlike June, he liked women as well as men. Maybe better than men, June didn't know and he didn't care. He wanted things to be good for him and wondered if that could happen if they stayed together.

James Kelly returned home without the slightly sallow look he'd had before going out. The vampire stuck to carefully planned circuit of people he paid for their blood. Not enough to do them any harm, but enough to keep him healthy and placid. He had not taken a life in a long time.

That had been all he'd wanted from June, a way to stop killing people.

He had gotten that, but he'd also ended up breaking up with his steady girlfriend, the woman who'd turned him into a vampire in the first place. They'd done more than break up, they'd severed ties altogether.

To June's knowledge, the relationship between a maker and their fledging tended to be strong, even if it wasn't romantic.

"Your mother called," June told him. "She's worried about you."

"She's always worried about me."

"I'd be worried if I hadn't heard from you in months."

James Kelly raised an eyebrow. "Are you feeling alright, June?"

A lie came to his lips, but he admitted, "No."

"Did you remember to eat?"

June had not remembered to eat; he'd been engrossed in his preparations for the upcoming trip. He had all kinds of things he'd need to bring with him so that he'd be able to perform the proper spells and rituals for his customers. But this was not that kind of feeling under the weather.

"You should eat."

The question jumped out before June had even thought about

it. "Am I ruining your life?"

"What?"

"Why won't you talk to your parents?"

"June..."

"Do you wish I was a woman?"

The vampire opened his mouth, then closed it. He glanced around the room. "I...No." He rubbed his nose, then repeated more firmly, "No."

"If you'd rather be with a woman—"

"June, don't. Don't say things like that."

"Why not?"

"Because..." He sighed, fidgeted then came to sit beside June on the couch. "Because I sort of depend on you not to. I need you to be the one telling me that this is alright, that we're not all those things people say we are."

June started to chew on his thumbnail.

"Cause you turn on the radio or the television and you hear all this about subversives and communists and being diseased."

June's stomach leaped into his throat.

"And you don't let it bother you—"

"Of course, it bothers me!"

"No, I mean, it makes you angry but it doesn't make you doubt. It doesn't make you think that you're really sick," James Kelly said, then asked, "Does it?"

"Not usually."

"Good. Don't let it."

June raised his eyebrows.

"You're not like the rest of us, you know. You've been around for so long, you've got such a broad perspective. It's a great line, being able to say that God made you a queer. I can't say that."

"You could if you wanted, I'm sure He wouldn't mind." June was not just being glib, he really didn't think the Almighty would mind those kinds of assertations at all.

James Kelly chuckled. "What's got you thinking about all this, anyway?"

June shook his head. "Don't worry about it. Forget I said anything. Have you decided if you're going to come with me?"

"I can't."

That was a change from not being sure. "Why not?"

"I haven't got any donors."

"Oh, that. You haven't got to worry about that, I know of a few places that have that sort of thing," June assured him. There was always someone willing to get bit if it meant a few more dollars in their pocket. "Or, you know, there's always me."

James Kelly shook his head right away.

"I really don't mind," June insisted. "I trust you, you know."

"No, I don't...I've got donors, I don't need to take anything else from you."

It became clear to June that he hadn't let the vampire know he wanted to do this as more than a favor, as more than another way to give him things. "I want you to."

He shook his head again. "You already give me too much."

"You don't understand," June told him, taking him by the hand. "I *want* you to. Like how I want you to kiss me."

His eyes widened. "Oh."

"If you want to bite me."

The vampire licked his lips. "I just drank."

June moved in and kissed him, not caring where this went but only knowing that he needed to feel his lips. Taking blood or heavy petting, June didn't care as long as James Kelly was the one doing it to him.

James Kelly wrapped his arms around June, pulling him closer. June took the chance to move on top of him, straddling the vampire and letting his hands find all his favorite places to caress. The other man responded in kind, kissing June's neck and biting, not the kind of bite for taking blood, but just for being frisky.

He had his hands crawling all over June's body, never staying in one place long, like he wanted to get a feel for everything and worried he wouldn't have time. His fingers found their way to the waist of June's jeans and untucked the plain t-shirt, then climbed across his stomach up to his ribs.

Kissing, June thought, was a wonderful thing and people should spend more time doing it. It had been so long since he'd had someone that was his to kiss all the time. Centuries, really. Sure, he'd had some fun and made it with a lot of good-looking men since his last serious relationship, but June liked this better. He liked coming home to someone. He liked knowing that in the morning, no one would throw him some lame excuse to leave.

He also liked when James Kelly would undo the fly of jeans, which he was doing now, sliding one hand inside June's pants. That hand gripped June at the hip, shying away from what he was really after. It always took him a few minutes to work up the courage to touch June and he never did it for very long.

Except today, once he'd wrapped his hand around June, he didn't pull back after his usual brief fondling. He kept going, sliding his hand back and forth, which made June push closer to him. It struck June as odd to be compelled so strongly by such a small act after so many years and partners.

His breath coming quick and not too far from being undone entirely, June let out a small moan. He couldn't think of a single thing he had ever wanted more than this. The vampire moved his hand faster and caught June's lower lip between his teeth.

June came and for a second, he couldn't think or remember where he was or what that sound was.

The phone, he realized hazily. He nestled his face into James Kelly's neck, feeling like he could melt.

"Oh!" He sat up straighter.

"What?" the vampire asked, his eyes going wide.

"Your mother!"

"...my mother?" he repeated.

"Your mother, I told her to call back," June said, reaching for the phone.

"June!" James Kelly hissed.

"Hi!" June answered.

"Hello. Is James Kelly around?"

"He is! Um...One second, I'll go get him." June placed the phone on the arm of the couch.

"I can't...!"

June tucked himself back into his jeans and grabbed the hand towel that hung off the oven door. He pressed it into James Kelly's hand and insisted, "Talk to your mother."

"I don't want to."

June leaned in close, almost on top of him again. He slipped his tongue into the vampire's mouth, then told him, "Talk to your mother." He picked up the receiver and placed it against James Kelly's ear.

"Hello," the vampire whispered, then cleared his throat and repeated, "Hello."

June pulled back.

"Yes, I'm fine. Yes, I'm sure. No, Momma..." He waited for a long time, fidgeting in his seat. "No, I...I don't want to meet..." He sighed, rubbed his eyes, and threw the hand towel on the coffee table. "No, I'm sorry, I will. Yes. I can't then, I'm going on a trip."

June raised his eyebrows and looked at the vampire, who looked away.

"We're going upstate. It's business."

June could not stop grinning and came over, perching on the edge of the coffee table, needing every bit of self-control to stop himself from climbing over and putting his ear next to the receiver.

"Yes. Yes. I promise I will. As soon as I get back. I love you. Say hi to Dad for me. I've got to go. I've got to pack. I love you. Goodbye." The vampire hung up the phone, looking like he'd been through a police interrogation. "Quit smiling."

"Are you really coming or did you just say that to get her off your back?"

"I'll come. She'll know if I don't, I swear to God she would."

"Of course, she would, she's your mother." June moved back to the couch and nipped at the vampire's earlobe, eager to pick up where they'd left off, badly wanting to have his turn to make James Kelly feel good.

James Kelly only sighed.

"What?"

He shook his head and stood, making his way to the bedroom, poking his head out a moment later to ask, "Have you seen my suitcase?"

"I threw it down the garbage chute."

He came all the way out of the bedroom, his arms crossed. "Why?"

"So you'd have to ask that."

"What?"

June examined his nails. "And then if you were looking for it I'd know if you were going to leave me."

"That's absolutely certifiable," James Kelly growled.

June looked up as James Kelly straightened out his clothes and stalked towards the door. Things had gone awry with haste and he hurried to say, "James Kelly, it's under the bed."

The vampire paused, glaring. "What?"

"I was only teasing, honey. I wouldn't do that."

He stood there, the wind gone out of him. "Oh."

"Come here."

"No, I was. That was stupid of me." He headed back to the bedroom. "I've got to pack."

June picked at his nails. He didn't know a lot about how things had been between Anastasia and James Kelly, but he had some suspicions, especially considering that she'd accused him of treason against all of vampire-kind just for breaking up with her.

He gave him some space, finishing his preparations for the trip, then made a sandwich. By the time he'd finished eating, James Kelly hadn't come out of the bedroom, so June went in. He didn't say or ask anything, just helped him get the suitcase packed.

The vampire broke their silence. "How much should I bring, anyway? How long are we going to be gone?"

"As long as you like."

"That's not an answer."

"Should be about..." June stopped to think. "Nine or ten days. Unless we want to make a detour somewhere. The last stop is right near these caverns and we can even do Niagara Falls if you want."

"I've been to Niagara Falls."

"Oh! How was that?"

"Well, it was...when I was eight my parents tried to send me to a Jewish sleep-away camp in the Catskills but when, um. When we got there the camp directors realized that the last name Rosenburg could belong to a colored boy, too." He shrugged. "They didn't let me in."

"Oh..."

"So we drove five hours to Niagara Falls instead. Didn't want to have rented a car for nothing, I guess."

June embraced him, knowing that there was nothing that could be done to make things better. "I've been told that summer camp is horrible."

"I'm sure I would have hated it. I never got to find out for myself, though."

Pressing a kiss to his cheek, June assured him, "You would have hated it."

James Kelly snorted.

MARCH 10, 1954.

Ten a.m. found June and James Kelly in a Long Island suburb, at the home of Paula and Bob Winston.

As June pulled the Rambler he'd borrowed from Wei into the driveway, James Kelly asked, "So who's this girl again?"

"Sissy is a friend of mine," June said.

"Yes, you said that. But who *is* she?"

"You remember that Halloween party?"

James Kelly hesitated to answer. "Yes."

"Remember the girl that hit you?"

"I do."

"That's Sissy," June told him, hoping it wouldn't set too bad of a tone for their trip. "But you know, you've got to keep in mind that after her mother died she spent years in one of those institutions for the mentally retarded."

"Oh."

"But she's not! I mean, the state went ahead and said she's an idiot, that she's the same as a three-year-old, but I know that's not true. I mean, she can *read*. What kind of three-year-old can read?"

"Uh-huh."

They sat, awkward and quiet, in the car for another half a

minute, before June got out and headed towards the door. James Kelly followed right behind, maybe not too keen on being alone in the middle of suburbia.

Bob and Paula greeted June warmly and smiled politely at James Kelly.

A pink-cheeked and blue-eyed girl poked her head into the foyer and June chided himself for thinking of her that way. She was a young woman, really, fully grown but whenever he looked at her he couldn't help but see the child that had always been curled up on her mother's lap, the toddler who had taken her first steps towards him.

She regarded James Kelly warily, her pale eyes flicking over him.

"This is my friend," June told her.

She looked at James Kelly's shoes.

"Are you ready to go?" June asked.

She nodded towards a trunk that had a beagle panting beside it. The dog's leash had been tied around one of the handles of the trunk.

"Gracie isn't coming," June reminded.

Paula sighed and untied the dog's leash.

"Come on."

Sissy didn't move.

Bob went for one handle of the trunk and said, "Son, you, uh, you mind giving me a hand with this?" to James Kelly.

June watched the vampire sidle over and help him lift the trunk.

Once they'd gone, June said, "Come on, Sis, you knew that Gracie couldn't come. We talked about it already."

She crossed her arms.

"Sissy, be a good girl," Paula insisted.

"Paula, it's fine. I'll wait. Maybe, uh, maybe you and Bob could just give us some time."

Paula hesitated. "I do have some Tupperware that I have to return to Helen..."

She clattered around in the kitchen and exited the house with pastel plastic containers cradled in her arms.

June had to wait for about five minutes before Sissy uncrossed her arms and looked at the door. "You ready?"

"No."

"Is it about Gracie or James Kelly?"

"Yes."

He took that to mean both. "Well, you knew you couldn't bring Gracie. And James Kelly won't bother you. He's nice. Do you want to say goodbye to Bob and Paula?"

"Already did."

"Do you want to say goodbye to Gracie?"

"Already did that, too."

He smiled and held out a hand. "Then come on, stop being difficult."

She didn't take his hand put wrapped her arms around him. She came all the way up to his shoulders. She squeezed him hard.

"Come on, Sis, tell me what it really is. I know you can."

"I don't like him." Hearing a full sentence from her still floored him. She'd spent so long hardly saying a thing and he hated to think of her in that place without anyone bothering to get a few words out of her.

He reminded, "You don't even know him."

"I want just us."

"Why?"

She tightened her arms around him but didn't answer.

"He's my friend."

She released him and headed out the door.

June watched as she let herself into the backseat of the Rambler. James Kelly and Bob still stood by the car, regarding each other uncomfortably.

"Go on," June told the vampire, "We'll be off in a second."

James Kelly got in the car and Bob came over to June. In a hushed voice and turned away from the car, he said, "Now, I know you mentioned about finding someone to help her out but Paula and I sort of thought you had meant a woman."

June couldn't help turning back to glance at the two in the car. "Oh. No. James Kelly is, well, he's my friend, not the help."

Bob squirmed. "Is that right?"

"After I drop Sissy off, I've got the rest of my upstate circuit to do so I thought, you know, it would be good to have company."

"Ah."

"And it is a woman," June said, "In Lily Dale. You haven't got to worry about that."

"Good, good."

"Anyway. I should be going. Long drive ahead."

"Of course."

June stepped away, not sure how he felt about the conversation, and climbed into the driver's seat. He fiddled with the radio for a while, trying to find something. He eventually settled on a soap opera.

"My mother listens to this," James Kelly told him.

June didn't know if it was a dig or not, so he didn't say anything in response.

"How far is it?"

"About eight hours I think."

From the backseat, Sissy hummed a show tune.

"Well, and I figured we'll have to stop somewhere for lunch. And then I don't know if there's traffic."

"Maybe not so much on Wednesday," James Kelly suggested.

"That's what I'm hoping." June kept one hand on the wheel but let the other crawl across the seat towards James Kelly's hand.

James Kelly moved his own hand away, placing it on his lap, and looked out the window.

"You, uh...you haven't got to worry about Sis, I don't think," June mentioned.

The vampire pressed his lips together, though June only knew because he could see it reflected in the window.

"Sis," June called.

She scooted forward to indicate that she was listening and gave James Kelly a bit of a look. She tucked a lock of dark brown hair behind her ear.

"Don't," James Kelly growled.

"It hasn't got anything to do with you, I can tell my business to whoever I want."

Sissy tapped June on the shoulder, her eyebrows quirked up.

"What do you know about homosexuals, Sis?"

"Perhaps as dangerous as the actual Communists are the sexual perverts who have infiltrated our Government in recent years," she quoted, her tone flat. "April 1950. Special to the New York Times—"

"Alright, fine," June interrupted. "What else?"

"I was a homosexual. An inside look at the 'gay' life, frankly told by a man who believed he was 'different' but conquered his unnatural impulses," she recited, "Real Magazine 1953."

"Christ, June," James Kelly huffed.

"And it's got...a picture about a sad man on it," she elaborated.

James Kelly glared at her.

June smacked the vampire with the back of his hand and shushed him. "Alright, then, where'd you read those?"

"At the library," she told him. "Pamphlets at the front desk, too."

He glanced at her, wondering if he should bother to say anything at all. "What if I told you I was one of those?"

"Pamphlet?" she asked.

He took his eyes off the road to see that she had a grin across her face. Apparently, learning to express herself also meant she'd learned to make jokes. "No," was all he could manage to say. He wanted to tell her that her mother had been funny, too.

"I know," she told him. She reached over the seat and squeezed his arm. "Not a pamphlet," she reassured him.

"But I am a queer."

"Junius Thompson, malak ha'satan, among the first fallen." She squeezed his arm again. "Queer as a three-dollar bill."

June chuckled, wondering where she'd picked up that expression. "You've got it, Sis."

"Honestly," James Kelly growled to himself. He'd moved as far away from June as he physically could in the car, pressed up against the passenger side door.

Sissy slid back into her seat, whispering-singing pretty as a lark, "You're every thought, you're everything, you're every song I ever sing." She hummed the rest of the tune to herself.

She didn't say anything else for hours, not until just before two fifteen in the afternoon when she tapped June on the shoulder and requested, "Perry Mason."

He obliged, turning the dial until he found the right station. It came in a little fuzzy and she leaned all the way into the front of the car to cast a spell on the radio. The fuzz cleared up right away and she beamed at him. She settled into the backseat but leaned forward with her arms hanging over the back of the front seat for the whole radio program.

"Have you read any of the books?" James Kelly asked.

She didn't answer, her eyes focused beyond the windshield.

James Kelly opened his mouth and June shook his head, holding up his hand in a gesture that he hoped indicated that James Kelly should wait a moment.

"Yes. I read the books," Sissy pronounced, her enunciation careful.

James Kelly looked astonished that she had answered him. He turned his gaze towards her, his eyebrows raised and his eyes wide.

She glanced in his direction, her cheeks slightly ruddier than normal. "I can read," she told him, her tone more defensive than might have been necessary.

"I believe you."

She jabbed him hard in the shoulder with one finger and returned to the backseat, her arms crossed again.

James Kelly frowned, first at her, then at June.

"Sissy, that's not nice," June scolded.

"Fuck. You."

June did not know what to say to that. He'd never heard her curse before, he'd never even imagined that she knew the words. Of course, he reasoned, most people thought she couldn't understand them, so she'd probably been exposed to a lot of bad language.

"Get out."

He glanced at her in the rearview mirror. "What?"

"I want get out of the car."

"We're not there yet," he tried to reason.

She screeched something that might have been the word no and June figured that pulling over would be the best bet. He didn't see any place that looked particularly appealing, so he pulled over to the right onto a grassy bank in the middle of nowhere, New York.

Better than the middle of nowhere, Pennsylvania, where they had been not too long ago. Something about Pennsylvania had never sat right with June and he blamed the Quakers, but he didn't think that was entirely fair.

More likely, though he hated to admit it, he didn't like Pennsylvania because it was where he had ended up after Georgia. After Georgia, he'd gone through a rough patch and Pennsylvania had provided the backdrop. He had been lost then, shambling through the days with few goals beyond food, shelter, and autonomy.

He shook those thoughts from his head. Dwelling too long in these kinds of dramatic, literary ideas would conjure the Devil more surely than any black mass.

When he'd parked and turned off the engine, he turned to look at Sissy.

She got out of the car without a word and headed off towards the copse of evergreens that bordered the embankment, her red wool jacket easy to see against the trees.

June got out too, but she turned back to him and held up her hand firmly to indicate that he should keep his distance.

He did.

She didn't go into the trees. She plunked down at the edge, facing away from him. He felt something tug at the energy that lurked below the surface of the visible world, a calm, steady flow moving in her direction. He leaned against the side of the Rambler and kept an eye on her, not thinking she would go anywhere but unable to stop worrying.

She was not a little girl, he reminded himself over and over. But he wanted her to be. He wanted her to have a childhood, a real one, but there was nothing he could do to fix how things had gone.

Sissy's mother would have been disappointed in him, he would have put money on it. He'd claimed to be her friend, but friends didn't let these kinds of things happen. There should have been something he could have done, even if it had meant he'd been breaking the law.

Which he had in the end, anyway. He'd taken Sissy from the school when she'd turned eighteen, but he'd done it without the right paperwork. It had been a mess for Paula and Bob to sort out, but June hadn't known there was paperwork involved in bringing her somewhere else. He'd been so worried about getting her out, worried that they wouldn't let a creature like him walk out with a young woman in his care.

James Kelly came out of the car to stand beside him, his hands in his pockets. "Should I not have said anything?"

"I don't know."

"I didn't mean anything by it."

"I'm not the one who's upset," June pointed out. "You've got to talk to her."

"I don't want to set her off again."

June shrugged. Yes, she'd gotten upset, but she'd also known what she'd needed to undo it and had been able to tell him what she needed. He hunched his shoulders, burrowing as best he could into the fleece lining.

The two of them leaned against the car side-by-side, their eyes fixed on the trees, pretending they weren't watching out her.

"Besides." June rubbed his nose and looked at his shoes.

"Besides what?" James Kelly prompted.

"I told her to be nice."

"You tell me to be nice all the time."

June sighed. "Is it bad that I want people to be nice to each other?"

"Absolutely horrendous, I have to tell you," the vampire teased.

June couldn't work up a smile.

Beneath his feet, a slow river of good feelings and quiet spaces made its way towards Sissy, winding through the Earth. Most witches her age couldn't tap into that energy. Drawing on the earth was something that took a lot of practice, along with a disposition for that kind of magic. Her mother had been that way with water, spending most of her time up to her knees in whatever river, pond, or ocean was closest, drinking in the tide.

A knuckle brushed the back of his hand, pulling June out of his memories.

James Kelly said, "What about Fred Astaire and Gene Kelly? Think we could do that of the number from *Ziegfeld Follies?*"

"You think they ever fucked?" June wondered, though he'd meant to keep the thought in his head.

"Fred Astaire's a Republican."

"But I heard Gene Kelly's wife is a Communist," June countered. "And you know what they say about Communists. Who would you rather make it with?"

"Rita Hayworth."

June was more surprised he'd gotten anything other than a scowl and blush out of the vampire. "Redheads, is that a predilection of yours?"

James Kelly shrugged. "I don't know. Is Judy Garland a redhead?"

"I'd say so."

"That's what my mother says, I always thought of her as a brunette. Anyway, that's just white women, isn't it? They've got to have something to make them interesting."

A grin fixed itself on June's face and he couldn't get rid of it. "You're a regular agitator, saying things like that."

James Kelly frowned a little and pushed his hands back into his pockets. "Well, you haven't got to—"

"No! It's a good thing. Agitate. God help us, someone's got to do it."

His brow still creased, he asked, "You really think that?"

"Sure, I'm always for a good civil rights movement. I helped Peggy paint about a thousand signs, I figure," June told him. "We can picket Washington."

"Now I know you're making fun of me."

"Don't you dare, James Kelly. I *saw* the dawn of mankind and they were all dark-skinned. I *never* held with any of this...race hatred, this white man's burden bullshit, e-especially not after—!" He stopped himself from going any farther. He didn't want to delve any deeper into these memories, not when it dredged up a queasiness that clogged his throat. "Let's talk about something else. Let's talk about Ginger Rogers some more."

"We weren't..." James Kelly trailed off and cleared his throat. He touched June's arm, longer than he ever normally would have outside of their apartment, at least ten whole seconds. He glanced up and suggested, "You should probably stop somewhere to eat. You haven't had anything for lunch. I bet she's hungry, too."

June's voice came out gurgling and thick with mucus, "I think there's a diner next couple of exits." He cleared his throat into the back of his hand. "We'll go when she's ready." He cleared his throat again and ground his knuckles into his eyes.

James Kelly put an arm around his shoulder and pulled him

into a one-armed hug. It felt like a hug he would give to a friend at a funeral. "I'm terrible with crying, so you'd better not start," he warned.

June nestled against his side.

"Do..."

"What?"

James Kelly shook his head. "Never mind."

"Please."

The vampire looked towards Sissy, still among the trees, then at the lack of cars on the highway. He sighed and moved away from June, scrubbing one hand over his neatly combed curls, disrupting their careful order somewhat. In a voice that would have been impossible to hear if they hadn't been somewhere still, he disclosed, "Sometimes I just...for no reason at all, I get this feeling like I'm going to...to turn inside out or something. Like the world might fall apart. And it...it never really goes away, not all the way. I can't remember *not* feeling this way."

June knew the feeling. "Time," he offered.

"What?"

"It fades after a while."

James Kelly picked up on the way he'd said it and guessed, "But it doesn't go away."

"I don't know."

"Makes me nervous when you don't know things."

"Makes me nervous, too," June told him.

James Kelly smiled. He let out a sigh and tilted his head back to look up at the sky. He lit a cigarette and June did the same. They smoked wordlessly until Sissy walked back over to them.

"Feel better?" June asked.

"Yes."

"Hungry?"

She thought for a moment, then nodded. "Yes."

June took a last drag and then stubbed out the butt of his cigarette, flicking it off to the side.

James Kelly decided to wait in the car. June hadn't been able to persuade him otherwise; he walked around to the other side of the car and tapped on the window to double check before he went inside.

James Kelly rolled down the window and assured, "I don't need to eat."

"Coffee?"

"No, thanks." He reached into the glove compartment and took out a well-thumbed copy of *Nineteen Eighty-Four*.

"How are you liking that?" June asked. Sissy tugged on his sleeve.

"Go eat," James Kelly told him and opened the book, not looking at June.

June had the overwhelming urge to lean all the way inside the window and put his tongue in the other man's ear. He didn't, but he thought about it for a while. He forgot when their waitress started openly ogling him, her eyes fixed on his horns the whole time both of them ordered.

She also brought him something different than what he had ordered, but he didn't point it out because a cheeseburger with cooked onions wasn't too different from a hamburger with raw onions.

Halfway through eating a club sandwich that she had picked apart, Sissy said, "Anne-Marie Sullivan."

"You know you can ask for no tomatoes." June nodded towards the slices she'd heaped on one side of her plate.

She speared them on her fork and deposited them on top of his French fries. "Don't change the topic."

"You know you're just like your mother. You look like her, too."

She looked up, her eyes narrowed and her lips pressed together. "No."

"You do. Especially those peepers."

Sourly, Sissy said, "She could talk."

"You can talk," he pointed out.

She snorted. "Not the right way."

He didn't know if he should assure her or let the statement lie, so he pushed the tomatoes off his food and grabbed a handful of fries, dredging them through ketchup. He shoved them in his mouth. "Annie-Marie Sullivan is fifty-seven, childless, with a bad case of arthritis in her hands. She's a third-generation hedgewitch that needs help putting her charms and potions together. You know, cutting, grinding, bottling."

Sissy wiggled her fingers at him. "I can do that."

"She's...a little brusque, but, you know, in that Yankee sort of way where she doesn't mean anything by it. Salt of the earth, maybe that's what I'm trying to say." He took another mouthful of fries. "I think you'll do fine together. I don't know her really well, but I've got a friend in Lily Dale who says she's swell. Respected. You'll be good for each other."

"Keeping an eye on me."

"Not like that, Sis. You've still got stuff you need to learn before you're on your own. And living alone...well, that's a big step. I don't think there's a lot of young women who'd be keen on moving to a new town and living alone."

"Maybe."

"And then when you've learned everything you need to know you can keep an eye on upstate for me."

She looked up. "Work with you?"

"Well, if you want. It's a husbandry school, isn't it? I

figured...see, Sis, I figured we'd work well together."

Sissy played with her straw. She hummed the entirety of "Anything Goes" then fiddled with the salt and pepper shakers.

"What?" he asked.

She shrugged and looked at him out of the corner of her eye, an odd smile on her lips.

"What?"

She pushed the straw to the other side of her drink.

"Come on, Sis, with that look."

"He lives with you?"

"Hmm?"

"He smells like you."

June gaped. "He lives with me," he confirmed.

"Used...I used to pretend that we would be like the story. With a princess and a castle. That you save me and I'm a grown up and live with you and we...I don't know. Happily ever after."

"Oh, I didn't..."

"I know. It was just pretend."

"I should have visited more."

She shrugged and June, who had seen a lot, had never seen a shrug that said so much. Loneliness and loss and heartbreak and forgiveness all in one noncommittal gesture. "I'm not yours."

He put his hand on the table, palm up, and she put her hand in his. "I wish things had been different."

She snorted and tapped her chest, making a face that said, without words, as much as he had felt bad about leaving her there, he had still done it.

"But Anne-Marie has a phone. You call me as much as you want. Collect."

She rolled her eyes.

"I mean it."

"Every day?"

"If you want," he affirmed. "And I'll visit."

"Birthday?"

He grinned. "Haven't missed one yet, have I?"

"Promise."

"I promise."

"June twenty-six," she told him.

"I know."

She tightened her hold on his hand. She ran one fingernail back and forth over her top lip over and over again.

When they walked back to the car, she tugged on his sleeve and asked, "Front seat?"

"Don't ask me," he told her.

She glanced at James Kelly, who still had his head bent over his book. She let out an irritated screeching noise.

"I thought we didn't do that anymore."

She poked June hard in the ribs.

"Hey," he warned. "One of these days someone's gonna poke you back." He walked away from her, getting in the car, leaving her to sulk outside and decide if she wanted to ask James Kelly or not.

The vampire looked up when the door closed and glanced outside. "What now?"

"What do you think about getting a dog?"

"It's a pretty small apartment for a dog."

"What about a small dog? A little Jack Russel or something."

"Is this going to be like getting a television?"

"I like dogs a good deal more than I like television."

James Kelly glanced outside again.

"Quit looking at her, she'll get in when she's ready."

"She won't take off or anything?"

"Hasn't yet," June said. Even as a child, Sissy had been more likely to clutch her mother's skirts than go wandering off. Maybe that had changed, but he thought Paula and Bob would have mentioned it. He leaned against the car door, turned so he could see her out of the corner of his eye.

Mostly he looked at James Kelly.

"What?" the vampire asked, squirming under his gaze.

"How's the book?"

"Fine. A little hard to follow sometimes with the way they talk and all."

June nodded. "It'll get you through the trip, though, I bet. We can pick up a paper and get you your crossword puzzle, too."

"I'd like to stop somewhere and get some postcards if you don't mind."

"Sure, no problem. Who've you got to send postcards to?"

"I should send one to my mother so she knows I wasn't lying."

"Doesn't she trust you?"

"Would you?"

"Trust you?"

"If you were my mother," James Kelly clarified.

"I don't know, how long did you wait to tell her you weren't dead?" June asked.

James Kelly half-shrugged. "Uh, well. I didn't know the Army had declared me dead, to be perfectly honest. I mean, it must have been a mistake. I was just about there anyway so when I went missing...they must have assumed someone else had wheeled me off in the night."

"No body, though," June pointed out.

"There were a lot of bodies, I figure they weren't worried about misplacing one like mine. Anyway, I called her...about a month after Annie changed me. I think she just about had a collapse."

"Mmm."

"I wanted to head back right away but..."

"But Anastasia didn't think it was such a hot idea?" June guessed.

"No, she said I needed more time control myself. And she wasn't wrong, I was a real beast then."

"I doubt that," June said. He had a tough time imagining James Kelly as one of the feral, blood-starved things that stalked alleyways and invaded homes.

But then again, the vampire had taken lives. June had come across him attempting it twice and had even seen the aftermath once.

"You didn't see me then," James Kelly told him. "But after a while, the idea grew on her and...well, to New York it was. She was like that. Once she got an idea in her head, she was going to get what she wanted."

"Mhm."

"As best I can explain it, that's why they let me get away with so much."

"I don't know, I'd let you get away with anything if you so much as smiled at me," June told him, smiling broadly.

Sissy rapped on the passenger window.

James Kelly rolled it down. "Uh. Can I help you?"

"I want front seat."

He stared at her for a second, maybe trying to untangle her abbreviated syntax. "Well. Uh. That's fine."

He took his book into the backseat with him. She climbed into the front and sat close to June, turning on the radio and searching for something with great intensity.

June cleared his throat and nodded towards James Kelly, but Sissy didn't take the hint. "What do you say?"

"Please."

He waited.

"Thank you," she corrected.

"You're welcome," the vampire told her.

She returned to the radio, finding a station she wanted to listen to before they'd pulled out of the diner parking lot.

June grabbed a map and handed it over his shoulder to James Kelly. "Give that a look over, will you, and double check what exit I need to take for Lily Dale."

After several minutes, James Kelly confirmed what exit he needed. June passed him back a copy of another book.

"I can't really read in the car."

"It's the *Green Book*. I thought you might want to glance through it."

James Kelly drummed his fingers on the cover. "You figure we'll get trouble?"

"I don't," June assured, "But you never know what's going to happen if we get a flat tire or something."

"Sure."

Guiltily, June considered that he hadn't told Anne-Marie Sullivan that he'd be bringing another person with him when he'd asked to use her spare room for the night. He hadn't even known when he'd made plans that James Kelly would come along and he didn't know how she'd feel about having an extra person around, especially one who was colored.

Certain types of witches tended to be of a progressive mind but others had positively antiquated stances. He could only hope that Anne-Marie would be the former.

"Besides," June said, then realized the lapse in their

conversation had been too long.

Sissy looked over at him.

"Hmm?" James Kelly asked.

"I wouldn't let, you know, I wouldn't let anyone do anything to you."

The other man cleared his throat. "Sure."

"I don't want you to worry."

"Alright."

June stopped talking, feeling sort of stupid and weirdly possessive of James Kelly. He tried to think of something else to say, something that could make James Kelly feel safe and secure. He couldn't and gave up after about half an hour.

"Sis."

"What?"

"Are you excited?" he asked, realizing he hadn't yet.

"I don't know."

He hadn't expected that answer. "You don't know? I thought you wanted to go here."

She thought for a long time. "To learn magic. Not...not because I want school."

"I understand."

She slid a little closer to him and rested her head against his arm. She let out a sigh and he reached over to pat her hand.

"What's the matter, Sis?"

"I want to be grown up."

June opened his mouth to respond but didn't think anything he said would be appropriate. He couldn't tell her that she was a grown-up because she'd missed out on so much she needed to learn. He couldn't confirm that she wasn't, because she was a young woman who should be able to determine her own path.

"I can't have with Bob and Paula."

"Why not?"

"They...they think I'm little in my head. Like a kid. Everyone thinks I am."

"Well—"

"You too!" she insisted.

"I try not to."

She pressed a little harder against him and he put an arm

around her. It wasn't the easiest way to drive, but he could deal with that for now. He hadn't done right by her, no one had, but maybe someday someone would.

She spent all of sunset staring out the window, her eyes fixed on the blood red sun as it sank. He wondered what she was thinking about, what she had thought about for all her years at Willowbrook or if she'd ever made any friends with the others there. If a single nurse had ever done her a kind turn.

"Lot of water around here," James Kelly commented.

"Wanna go for a swim?" June asked.

The vampire snorted. "Sure, I already died once, hypothermia won't be able to get me."

"Not dead," Sissy corrected.

His eyes widened, which they did any time Sissy addressed him directly. "Well, no, not really. But I died."

She turned her eyes away from the last sliver of sun and faced him. "What's it like?"

"To die?"

She nodded.

June felt immediately he should scold her but held his tongue. The conversation was between the two of them and if James Kelly wanted to tell her off, he could certainly manage it on his own.

At first, he didn't think James Kelly was going to answer her, but slowly, he said, "I was sick first. Pneumonia. I couldn't get out of bed, couldn't stop coughing or shaking. That kind of coughing where your ribs and stomach muscles hurt. I felt like I was dying, I mean. I *was* dying. So when Annie came and drained me...it felt just like I had the whole time. Weak and cold and *tired*."

Sissy had turned all the way around, kneeling on the seat and resting her forearms on the edge.

June drove by the house he was supposed to stop at and had to turn down a street and loop back around.

"While I was dead...you ever know you had a dream but when you wake up you can't remember what it was about?"

"Yes."

"It was like that. I felt unsettled about it for the longest time. Sometimes..."

"What?" she prompted.

"Sometimes I guess it comes back to me in little bits while I'm sleeping. Or I think it does. I don't know."

This time, June pulled into the driveway of a Folk-style Victorian that appeared navy in the darkness, but would probably prove to be a lighter shade of blue when the sun rose again. "Here we are."

There was a light on in the living room.

June cleared his throat and suggested, "Uh. Why don't you two start getting Sis's stuff, I'll go on in and let her know I'm here."

Neither of them moved, but June had to, rushing towards the house with his hands shaking. James Kelly's story about dying had unnerved him more than he'd expected and now that the moment came to leave Sissy with a stranger, he felt particularly unsteady.

Anne-Marie was a steady, sensible woman who'd taken on other boarders. She had patience and that gruff Yankee kindness that would do Sissy well. This would be a good place for the young witch, a place for her to learn and grow and be safe.

He told himself this a half-dozen times between the car and the front porch.

He knocked on the door, not sure if this was the right thing. Every fiber of him said that he should bring Sissy back to Manhattan with him, though to do what, he didn't know. Take care of her. Make sure she was happy and healthy and loved. To stop her from having to grow up and do grown-up things.

A young man, slight of frame with doe eyes, answered the door and stared at June. He closed the door halfway and asked, "Uh, what, what can I do for you?"

"Is this Anne-Marie Sullivan's house?"

He knew it was but he hadn't expected anyone else to answer the door. He briefly entertained the idea that the witch had moved without telling him.

The young man nodded.

"She's expecting me. You can tell her Junius Thompson is here."

"Oh, uh...Nan had to go out, down to see Mrs. Gallagher about the twins but...well, she's expecting you?" The young man stared at June. "You're all blue, you...uh, you sick or something, mister? I don't know if Nan can help with that kind of sick."

"I...no." June reached into his bomber jacket and took out his most recent letter from Anne-Marie and handed it over to him. "She's taking on another witch to help out."

"Oh." He took the letter and gave it a read over; either he read it several times or he was a slow reader. After a while, his face relaxed and said, "You know, I sort of remember her saying something about taking on someone new, now that I think about it." He peered past June towards the Rambler. "Well, she said she'd be back a little late. Why don't you all come in?"

"Well, uh. What's your name?"

"Oh, gee, I'm sorry!" He held out a hand for June to shake.

June noted the pale brown color of the skin as they shook hands. Light but not so light that a person couldn't tell he had African heritage.

"My name's Greenie. Well. Folks call me Greenie but my name is Kerry Greene. My momma always gets mad when I let people think that's what she named me."

June smiled. "Nice to meet you. You, uh..."

"I work for Nan sometimes. Things around the house and yard. She rang me up, asked me to come over and feed the dogs, though. I live right down the street."

"I see."

James Kelly approached, carrying Sissy's trunk. "Where do you want this?"

June and Greenie looked at each other and the young man said, "You can put it right inside the door."

He stepped back and opened the door wider to make room.

James Kelly carefully edged inside the door and set down the trunk. It settled against the hardwood floor with a *thunk* and Greenie noted, "Gee, sounds heavy!"

June gestured for Sissy to come inside, which she did, eyeing Greenie the whole time.

Once inside, June spied three large dogs of mixed heritage sitting in the living room to the left of the entrance. The largest was a shaggy white beast; the other two were smaller but of a similar size to each other, a brown and black shepherd mix and a sleek-coated light brown dog with the look of a pit bull. None of them moved much, except to shift a paw or wag their tail.

"Don't worry, they're friendly!" Greenie assured. "And they listen."

Sissy stared at the dogs.

"You like dogs, miss?" Greenie asked her.

She beamed, still looking at the dogs. "Yes."

That she'd said anything at all to the young man surprised June.

Greenie went into the living room, ruffled the fur on the largest dog's head. "This is Galahad." He patted the side of the shepherd mix, which had one floppy and one upright ear. "This is Desdemona and this one," he said with a nod towards the sleek one, "Is Jimmy Olson."

James Kelly looked over, his brow furrowed. "Like from the comics?"

"Sure!" Greenie eagerly answered.

"I can pet them?" Sissy asked.

"Of course, miss," Greenie told her.

She came into the living room and spread her arms. The dogs broke rank, circling around her to investigate, sniffing and nosing at her, licking her fingers. She knelt among the dogs and they started lapping at her face. The dogs' attention elicited giggles and coos of happiness from the young woman and June couldn't help the grin that spread over his face.

"Guess she does like dogs, huh?" Greenie said to James Kelly.

James Kelly nodded.

"Can I get you something to drink? Some water or maybe some coffee?"

The four of them migrated to the kitchen, the dogs following behind Sissy, collapsing around her feet as she sipped at a glass of apple juice.

June stirred his coffee and watched James Kelly restrain himself from shoveling in as much sugar as he normally did. June had to restrain himself from playing footsie with him under the table. His presence alone was always a terrible temptation and now, disquieted as June felt, he wanted the vampire's skin against his.

"If it's not too nosy, what's got you coming to Lily Dale, miss?" Greenie asked.

She looked at him, licked her lips, and set down the juice glass.

"Canadensis."

"I'm sorry?"

"My name is Canadensis. Not miss."

"That's a respectable witch name, miss!" the young man crowed.

She frowned slightly.

"Oh, I'm sorry, but that's...well, my momma made sure I had good manners."

"Sissy just gets a little particular about things," June explained, though she didn't look happy that he'd said anything. He sipped his coffee and tried to mind his own business.

"What's your name?" she asked the young man.

"Kerry Greene, but most people..." he trailed off as someone else entered the house.

They all turned to see a woman enter, her dark hair in a neat braid, her dress plain and spattered with what must have been a potion or poultice, because she brought a strong scent of herbs with her.

The dogs all started wagging their tails.

She came into the kitchen and June stood, offering her his hand. "Junius Thompson, malak ha'satan—"

"I remember you, Mr. Thompson. Forty-nine, wasn't it? That business with the fish kill."

He nodded. "It was."

"And this is Canadensis Walsh, as best I can figure," she said, looking at Sissy. "And that...?"

"James Kelly Rosenburg," the vampire said, standing and offering his hand.

She didn't take it. Her eyes went from warm and kind to cold and hard just from looking at James Kelly. "You let him in?" she asked Greenie.

James Kelly pulled his hand back, his shoulders hunching and his eyes sliding towards June. He swallowed once and then the hurt on his face melted away, replaced with a smooth, easy look of not acceptance but confirmation. He had expected this from the start.

He always expected this, June realized.

Greenie flushed and rubbed the back of his neck. "I didn't want to be rude."

"I know you'd said I could stay the night and if it's not too much trouble we were—" June began.

Anne-Marie cut him off, "I'm sorry, but my answer's going to have to be no. I just won't have his sort under my roof. I hope you understand."

"I'm afraid I don't," June told her, trying to keep his voice even.

"A woman living alone has to be careful, you know, and I'm not about to stop being careful."

June's instinct was to say that James Kelly had never hurt anyone, but it wasn't true. He had killed and more than once.

But not without need, June reminded himself, and he had no need now.

"I don't normally truck with demons, either, but Jeanine Lance says that you're a decent sort," Anne-Marie informed him.

James Kelly started to laugh, a full-body laugh with a hysterical edge. He clapped one hand on June's shoulder and used the other to cover his mouth like he was trying to push the laughter back into his mouth.

Anne-Marie didn't seem to understand what was so funny.

James Kelly walked out of the kitchen, heading out of the house.

June hesitated, then insisted to Anne-Marie, "He won't hurt you."

"I'm not taking chances. His nature is killing," she pronounced with finality, her hands set firmly on her hips.

June shook his head. "It might be part of the condition but it's not his nature." That he would stake his life on. "And besides, he's got it managed."

"How long has he been dead for?"

"Since forty-five, I think."

"And when was the last time he'd killed someone?"

It had been more than a year. He remembered the last time the vampire had killed someone, his addled state when he'd show up at June's apartment, smeared with blood. "He didn't know any better," he insisted. "He never got taught the right way."

"I've put my foot down."

"Well..." He glanced around the kitchen, not looking for

anything but needing to look somewhere other than Anne-Marie's sensible face. Vampires could be dangerous and beyond any actual threat they posed, they had a terrible reputation; he couldn't expect the witch to set aside everything she knew on his word alone. Not on the word of a demon. "Can you at least tell me somewhere in town we can stay?"

"Can't think of a place around here that's keen on his type."

Greenie shifted nervously.

Sissy grabbed on to June's sleeve. "You stay."

He put his hand over hers. "Sis, I can't, not without him."

She swallowed, her eyes glittering.

"My momma...well, we've got room of a sort. I could make a phone call," Greenie offered. "Let me give her a call."

"Please. I'd appreciate that."

Greenie went over to the phone and June tried to step away from the kitchen table. Sissy held hard onto his hand.

June extracted himself from her grip. "I'll be right back. Why don't you and Anne-Marie talk a little bit, get to know each other?"

She pressed her lips together and nodded wordlessly.

He gave her shoulder a squeeze then headed out. As he walked outside, he heard Anne-Marie tell Sissy to wash her face and then they would talk.

June found the vampire leaning against the Rambler, smoking.

"You better watch out, being seen with the likes of me," James Kelly warned. "It'll ruin your reputation for sure."

"I didn't figure..." June sighed. "I'm sorry."

He shrugged. "One more thing for people not to like. Nothing I can do about it."

"Greenie says he'll ask his mother."

"Better than the car." He stubbed out his butt and left it on the driveway. Without asking, he reached inside June's jacket and took his pack. He stared at the three in there.

"You can have them."

James Kelly lit one and held it out to June, then lit another for himself when June had taken it. He stowed the last one.

"I feel fucking awful about this," June confessed. He took a drag.

With his eyes on the ground, James Kelly proposed, "Let's not talk about it anymore."

June leaned beside him.

Neither of them spoke for a while. The evening had a lot of sounds, crickets and the gentle rustle of branches in the wind. Voices floated down the street, a man and a woman, young by the sounds of it and besotted with each other.

The couple passed by Anne-Marie's house, two clean-cut young people walking hand in hand. They glanced towards the pair of men in the driveway and June raised his hand in greeting.

They didn't return it but hurried their pace; the woman giggled nervously after a few feet.

When they'd passed further down the street, James Kelly asked, "Is it that easy to tell what I am?"

"Witches have a sense for things like that sometimes," June explained. "They feel things other humans can't always feel."

"And...never mind."

"Go on."

"What do vampires feel like? I know when I see another one it's just this sort of...suspicion. Like I'm not exactly sure, but if I had to put money on it, I know which way I'd go."

"I don't know what witches feel but I know when I see a vampire I usually get the sense that, uh, that all of them doesn't quite belong together. Like you've got your own sort energy that makes up you and then there's this...human bit humming through you. It's stronger right after you feed and then things sort of meld."

"Oh."

"Kind of like when you move a plant or something, the soil needs time to marry." June made a mixing gesture with his hands that he hoped illustrated his point.

James Kelly nodded, his eyes on his shoes.

June wanted him to look up. He wanted to take him somewhere perfectly dark where there would be a million stars.

Greenie came out. "Uh, I talked to my momma."

They both looked at him.

"She says, well, we've got a detached garage and it's got a couch. My brother used to sleep out there when him and Pop were at it...got a sink too, so you can wash up. She figures letting you into the garage isn't the same as letting you into the house."

"Figure it'll be better than sleeping in the car," James Kelly said.

"Right, well, I'm going to say goodbye to Nan. Then I'll walk you over."

When they were alone, James Kelly asked, "Should I tell them I can go inside without being asked?"

"I wouldn't, otherwise they might start chaining you up in coffins."

James Kelly rolled his eyes.

"I'd kind of been hoping that we might get to share the spare room though." June took a chance and ran his hand down the vampire's arm.

James Kelly shook his head and took half a step away.

Greenie came back out and said to James Kelly, "I'm right across the street, come on."

As they walked away, James Kelly asked him, "You really let people call you Greenie?"

"Sure. You don't have any nicknames?"

"If my mother had wanted people to call me something else, that's what she would have named me."

Greenie laughed. "If you weren't dead, my momma would like you!"

June watched them go, finished his cigarette, and went back inside.

Anne-Marie showed both of them to their rooms and June helped Sissy lug her trunk upstairs, which would have been easier if the three dogs hadn't been so intent on helping, too.

They ate, all three of them more or less quiet the entire time, and when the dishes had been done, June claimed exhaustion from driving all day.

He waited until the house went quiet and dark and then waited another hour. It was, according to his watch, just after one a.m.

He climbed out the window, reminded of a time in the third century, except then he'd been fleeing from people he'd owed a lot of money. He crossed the street, relishing the bite of the cold air on his cheeks. He found the window of the attached garage and tapped his claws against the glass.

About a minute passed before James Kelly came over and opened the window. "What are you doing?"

June shrugged. "You going to invite me in or not?"

"I was sleeping."

"I couldn't."

James Kelly looked him over. "Come around to the door."

June scampered over to the door and as soon as it was open threw his arms around James Kelly. "You smell like gasoline and old cardboard."

"You smell like cabbage."

"God help me, I had to eat it, she wouldn't let me say I wasn't hungry." He started undoing the buttons on James Kelly's pajama shirt.

James Kelly pushed June's hands away and closed the door.

"I like these pajamas."

"They're yours."

June slid his hands around James Kelly's waist, unable to find the words to express how much he liked the idea of James Kelly wearing his pajamas.

"Stop unbuttoning me, it's cold in here."

He stopped undoing buttons but offered, "I'll find a way to keep you warm." He put his lips to the vampire's throat.

"Well, don't light any fires, I don't want to go up in flames." James Kelly took him by the hand and gave him a tug. "Come over to the couch."

June settled in next to him and took the blanket from the couch, throwing it around the vampire's shoulders.

While he was doing that, James Kelly kissed him. "Thanks for coming over."

"I wanted to make sure you were all set."

The vampire shifted, then shrugged. He rebuttoned his pajamas.

"What?"

"It was a long day."

"Mmm," June agreed and wound his arms around him, resting his head on his shoulder. "You can go back to sleep. I'm sorry I woke you."

"Come under the covers." James Kelly opened his arms and June nestled up to him, not being as careful as he should have with his horns. The vampire yelped and June tried to pull away, but James Kelly tightened his grip. "Don't go goring me for nothing, you stay over here."

"I'm awfully sorry."

"Barely poked me, really. I was teasing." James Kelly kissed

June's temple, then ran his fingers over June's horns, tracing the shape. "What came first, you or mountain goats?"

"Shut up."

The vampire kissed his cheek.

June shifted a little. "They're *not* goat horns." Goat horns stuck up. His horns curled, staying more or less close to his skull. Much more ram than goat, everyone who knew anything about animals agreed. A city boy like James Kelly couldn't be expected to know that, though, and June figured he had to forgive him for the poor comparison.

The vampire caught June's earlobe between his thumb and forefinger. "You ever headbutt anybody?"

"Maybe once or twice."

James Kelly giggled.

"What?"

"I can't imagine you doing anything like that."

"You think I'm a lot nicer than I am," June told him, "Everyone does. There's that idiot June with all his plants."

"I don't think that," James Kelly assured. "I've never seen you do a single bad thing to anyone, though."

June squirmed, thinking of the run-in he'd had with Anastasia; he'd nearly killed her over nothing and he'd needed to call his king to make things right. He hadn't ever mentioned it to James Kelly any more than he'd ever mentioned the things that had happened in Georgia or any of the things before that. "I've done them, don't you worry."

James Kelly said nothing else and June started to drift off, lulled by the vampire's gentle fingers tracing through his hair and over his horns.

"How long are we going to be here?"

"Hmm?" June's eyes blinked open with some difficulty.

"In this town."

"Oh. Leaving tomorrow afternoon, I figure. I've got to do something for this orchard that's...east? West. West of here. And then we're off."

"Do you think a lot of people will be able to figure out I'm a vampire?"

"No, I don't think so, none of the rest of the stops have

witches or anything, at least not until we get to the festival. But there will be all sorts there, probably even other vampires."

"I don't know how people don't give you more trouble." He had his fingers running over June's horns again.

"Sometimes they do. Mostly I think they're too surprised. Used to be worse, when people were more superstitious. Used to always keep a hood up, pretend I was a monk if I had to go somewhere that I didn't know."

"What I wouldn't give to see that!"

"I'll play dress up for you if you'd like," June offered in his smoothest voice.

James Kelly chuckled and pulled him even closer, as close as he could get without being inside him. His lips grazed June's jaw. "I'd rather have you taking things off for me than putting them on."

"Don't tease me like that," June purred, twisting in the vampire's arms and pressing a kiss to his mouth. He soon realized that the use of the word 'tease' had been a grave miscalculation.

James Kelly tensed up.

"No, I didn't...I didn't mean...shit, I'm sorry."

The vampire shook his head and placed his hands on June's shoulders, pushing himself back more than he was pushing June away. He swallowed and swept his hands over his face, leaving them to rest on his lap. The blanket slipped from his shoulders.

He was so young, June thought. He'd only lived to be twenty-one and it showed. He looked like a kid and June felt like a fool. "James Kelly."

"Maybe you should go."

"I don't want to."

"Go find someone else that's what you think I'm doing."

June assured, "I think you're doing the best you can."

"But it's not good enough for you, you—"

"Don't," June cut off his snarling. "Don't start calling me names. I won't stand for it."

That took the vampire aback somewhat and he stared at June, his golden eyes puffy and reddened.

"You get mean when you're scared, you know, and it hurts."

"I'm *always* scared."

"I know." June reached over to arrange the blanket around

him again. "But you haven't got to be scared when you're with me."

"I'm sorry." The words came out with a tremble and June thought his heart would just about break if a single tear skated its way down the vampire's cheek.

"You haven't got to be sorry, either. You've just got to be you." He put his hand on the side of James Kelly's face.

He shook his head and pulled away from June's touch.

"Yes," June insisted. "I love you, kid, alright?"

James Kelly didn't look at him. "Don't call me 'kid'."

"I love you, James Kelly. I love you like the moon loves the stars."

"What's that even mean?" he grumbled.

"It means a lot, doesn't it? They're always hanging around together up there, aren't they?" He scooted a little closer to the other man. "You didn't really want me to go, did you?"

"No," he admitted.

"You should stop doing that, telling me to go when you want me to stay. Or walking away and wanting me to follow."

"No, I learned my lesson about doing *that*."

"It's a good way to get a guy confused, I'll give you that, but it isn't great for getting one to stick around," June said. He slid his fingers against the vampire's hand and twined their fingers, blue and brown, together. He let out a bit of a laugh. "Not like I'm looking for you to give me a reason to stick around, I'd probably still be tripping over myself and fawning over you even if you were mean to me and storming off all the time."

"Why?"

"Cause I love you, dummy, I told you already," June said with a grin.

James Kelly cracked a smile, which he normally would if June kept at it.

"Let's get some sleep, anyway. It is awfully chilly in here, good thing I came over to keep you warm."

It wasn't a perfect fit, the two of them on that lumpy couch, but June didn't mind. James Kelly snuggled up to him, his hands buried in the fleece lining of June's jacket and his legs curled so his feet didn't poke out from under the blanket. Underneath the smell of moldering cardboard and gasoline, June could smell soap and aftershave and cigarette smoke.

June woke up feeling overheated and greasy and generally unpleasant. He thought, at first, he'd woken because of this sensation, but realized it had been because of the sound of someone opening the garage door.

Greenie stood just inside the door, his hand still on the knob, his eyes fixed on the two of them. He had a bundle of sheets under one arm.

James Kelly would never let this go, June knew right away. Being caught would spoil any chance he ever had of being comfortable; if he was going to be seen with another man, it had to be on his terms.

Which probably meant he had to be drunk or fifty years in the future.

June and Greenie stared at each other.

The young man wiggled his arm holding the sheets and whispered, "I...I uh. I thought I should cover up the window, maybe? To stop the sun coming in."

June tried to find the right words but started to worry as James Kelly stirred.

"Anyway. I. I'll leave these." Greenie set down the sheets and scooted back out the door.

James Kelly stretched and yawned. "What was that?"

"What was what?"

"I thought I heard something."

"No."

The vampire sat up and rubbed his eyes. "What time is it?"

"About dawn, I figure," June answered, gauging his answer by the weak, gray light coming through the window.

"Maybe you should get back before anyone wonders where you got to."

"Sure. I'll see you in a little bit." June wanted to kiss him but didn't risk it.

He found Greenie bringing in the newspaper. "Hey."

The young man glanced his way and froze up. "Uh. What?"

"Don't, you know, say anything to anyone."

"I don't even know what I would say, to be honest," the young man admitted.

"Nothing, if you're smart."

Greenie stared, his doe eyes wide enough that June worried they might fall right out of his face.

"I'm not going to do anything to you. He's sensitive about it, is all."

"Sure."

They stared at each other for a second.

"But it's not true, then, I guess, what people say about you?" Greenie asked.

"Well, no, I'm not much for communism."

Greenie frowned and June figured the quip must have flown right over his head.

"What do people say about me?" June asked.

"That you're a confirmed bachelor."

June couldn't help but frown. "How do you figure?"

"I mean...the two of you...?"

"It's a euphemism," June explained.

"That's not any of my business, really." Greenie put up his hands to ward off any more perceived oversharing.

June ached for a cigarette but he'd smoked his last one waiting for everyone to go to bed last night. "When people say someone's a confirmed bachelor, they're saying he's a fag without having to get their mouth dirty with a word like that."

"Really?"

"Really."

"Then it is true, I guess. That you're one of those."

June glanced towards the horizon. A glance at his watch confirmed that it was just after six. "Anywhere open this early? I need a smoke."

"Not strictly speaking, but Pop will let us in. Come on."

Greenie set off down the street and June followed him. The younger man started chattering about how his grandfather owned a general store and proudly declared that Greene's was the only store owned by colored man for a hundred miles at least. June didn't doubt it.

"Three generations. I'll be four. Isn't that something?"

"Sure is."

Greenie unlocked the door of the general store and held it

open for June so he could go in first.

A gray-haired man of about sixty-five had his back to the door, stocking the shelves but when June stepped inside, he turned around, scowling at June.

"How'd you get in here?" he demanded.

June glanced back towards his companion.

"I don't want no trouble."

"Pop," Greenie scolded good-naturedly. "This is Junius, he's staying with Nan. He wants to buy a pack of cigarettes."

"You know how to work the register."

Greenie rolled his eyes and went over to the counter. June nodded towards the pack he wanted, then said, "Actually, can I get two?"

"Sure, anything else?"

June shook his head. "No, thanks." He handed over a dollar and pocketed the change.

"Since you're here," Pop said.

"Momma's got me doing chores at the house."

"Come back when you're done."

"Yes, sir."

As they walked back, June lit a cigarette and offered one to Greenie, who declined. "I think my momma would just about kill me if I did."

June returned the pack to his jacket. "How old are you?"

"Seventeen."

June took a drag. "You're about Sissy's age."

Greenie looked over too quickly, color coming to his cheeks. "She came to study at Ms. Goodespeake's school, right?"

"Sure did."

"Lots of people come up to do that. Most of them don't actually know a thing about witching, though. Ms. Goodespeake sends half of them packing in a month."

"Sissy's a proper witch," June assured him.

"That's what I figured. Canadensis. That's a good witchy name. She doesn't talk much, does she?"

June shrugged. "She'll open up when she gets to know you."

"You think so?"

"Sure. Give her time."

Greenie smiled.

They parted ways outside Greenie's house. June made his way back upstairs to shower.

He crossed paths with Anne-Marie in the kitchen. She glanced him over. "How'd you sleep?"

"Fine, thanks. Need help with anything?"

"Nope. Coffee's over there. Food'll be up soon."

He poured himself a mug of coffee and settled in at the kitchen table. "You, uh, how'd you and Sis get along?"

"She'll do fine. Doesn't talk much."

"Mmm."

"I like that in a girl. Too many girls just want to chatter all day long."

June drank his coffee black, too intimidated by Anne-Marie to ask for sugar or milk.

Sissy came downstairs and June wondered if the scent of bacon had pulled her from bed. She looked sleep-rumpled and disoriented.

He held out a hand to her and she took it. "How're you?"

She shrugged.

"Coffee?"

She grimaced.

After breakfast and dishes, June went upstairs with Sissy and helped her unpack. They did it without speaking. Around ten, everything had been unpacked and they still hadn't said a word.

He looked at his watch. He had appointments to keep. He'd known he wouldn't be able to stay with her for long. Two of the dogs, the big white one and the sleek one, lay on the floor, their tongues lolling contentedly out of their mouths.

She looked at the clock.

"I've got to go."

She shook her head. "Stay."

"I can't, Sis."

She threw her arms around him and squeezed him hard. "Please."

He hugged her back and kissed her hair. "You're going to be alright."

She shook her head.

"You will, I promise. You're smart and strong and you're going to learn so much."

She let out a sob.

"I'll call you. And you'll call me."

"Visit?"

"Absolutely."

One of the dogs nosed its way between the two of them, panting happily.

"Besides, now you've got *three* dogs."

She didn't seem comforted by that. She sniffled, then started to cry, clinging to him the whole time. He held her until she'd cried herself out.

He got her to wash her face and drink a glass of water, then he said, "I really have to go now."

"Love you."

"I love you, too, Sis. Want to walk me downstairs?"

She shook her head.

He understood. He kissed her forehead and left her with the dogs.

He found Anne-Marie in the kitchen washing herbs at the sink. He said, "I'll call to check in."

The woman glanced up from her work, then nodded.

"Thank you for letting me stay."

"Welcome."

"Go easy on her, you know? It hasn't been easy for her."

She scowled at him. "It's not easy for anyone."

"She's not like other people. She's sensitive."

The woman ceased working, wiped her hands, and turned to face him. "You told me that when we first talked. If I'da wanted you to repeat it, I woulda asked. You got places to be and that vampire's been hanging around my driveway waiting for you."

He went without another word and found James Kelly leaning against the Rambler.

"I could use a smoke."

June handed over the unopened pack of cigarettes he'd bought and climbed into the front seat, backing out the driveway, and heading off towards the apple orchard. He knew the way there pretty well; he'd been there every couple of years for the past three decades or so.

"You alright?" James Kelly asked. "You haven't said a word to me."

June didn't know what to say, so he shrugged and grunted.

MARCH 11, 1954.

The Dupre family owned a ninety-acre orchard and had since before the Civil War. They had been one of the first families to call on June's services after he'd relocated from Scranton to Manhattan at his king's behest.

He had spent his first decade or so in Manhattan skulking around and generally feeling sorry for himself until he'd started living with Wei a little before the Great War. Wei, enterprising as he was, usually had his fingers in two or three pies. Thirty years ago, Wei had been buying hard cider from the Dupre family, until they'd had trouble with some of their trees. June had volunteered to go up and fix things. It had spiraled from there, peaking with a multistate evasion of police in a stolen 1923 McFarlan and concluding in the bed of a very cute blond.

Memories of that cute blond flared up as June nosed the Rambler down the long dirt drive that would bring him to the farmhouse. Normally, he would have shared the story with James Kelly, not to make him jealous but because it was a fun story to tell. Now, though, the memories only made June morose, no matter that it had been a fantastically good time with Gerald or Gerhart or Gilbert or whatever his name had been.

June hadn't said a thing since they'd left Lily Dale and after the first few times asking, James Kelly had given up.

Now that the old farmhouse loomed in front of him, June felt bad for not saying anything. "We're not staying here tonight."

James Kelly looked over in his direction.

"It'll only take a couple hours."

The vampire nodded.

"You can come watch if you want."

James Kelly peered out the window towards the half-dozen people who had come out of the farmhouse. "You don't think they'll mind me hanging around?"

"If any of them can tell the difference between a vampire and a hole in the ground..." June started but didn't know how to finish. He got out of the car, fetched one of his suitcases from the trunk, and clicked his claws on the windshield when James Kelly didn't follow.

The vampire lingered behind him as they approached the farmhouse. Three more people had come out since he'd pulled up, including two small girls, one about three and the other maybe eight.

The older child yanked on the sleeve of Milton Dupre and demanded, "Daddy, is that an African!"

Milton hushed her and said to his wife, "Dolly, go on, get the girls inside."

The girl, however, couldn't be corralled by her mother and clattered down the front steps, coming right up to June and asking the same question of him.

He greeted her pointedly, "Hello, Prudence."

She rolled her eyes. "Hi. Well. Is he?"

"He's from Brooklyn."

She looked disappointed. "That's not Africa at all." She peered around June at James Kelly. "You sure? My encyclopedia says that Negros come from Africa."

James Kelly, judging by the almost contained smile on his face, was more amused than upset so June said, "Why don't you go ask him? I've got to talk to your dad."

Prudence didn't need to be told twice and ran right over to James Kelly, the sun lighting up her brown hair with hints of gold and caramel.

Milton's hair had looked like that before it had all fallen out. June approached him and shook hands with the man.

"Come on in, now, get yourself settled."

From inside the house, Dolly asked him if wanted something to eat or drink. He declined. They made small talk for about two minutes, then Milton cleared his throat and said, "We'll leave you to it."

They would clear out of the house, June knew, and avoid him while he walked the land to work his rites and spells. They were, generally, God-fearing folk and liked to know as little about his work as they could. As long as his work kept their orchard healthy and didn't involve sacrifices, their immortal souls, or invoking the Devil, they were content to pay for his services and part ways.

He headed into their kitchen, setting his suitcase on the table. As he unfastened it, he realized that someone had followed him in.

He glanced over to see the eldest Dupre girl hovering in the kitchen doorway. "Hi there, Edna."

"Uh, hi there, Mr. Thompson. How are you?"

"I'm fine, thanks. You?"

She bit her lip and looked at her penny loafers. "I'm alright."

"Can I help you with something?" he asked, taking into account the false ring to her answer the way she kept her eyes anywhere but on his face.

"If, uh, when you're done with the trees…I've kind of got something I need help with. If you don't mind. I've got some money saved and everything."

She was twenty-one or twenty-two if June guessed right, and normally girls of that age wanted a specific kind of help from June. Either to end or prevent unwanted pregnancies. He thought he recalled her getting married at some point, but he could have been mistaken. Or things could have not worked out with her mister. "Sure."

She gave a nervous smile. "Thanks. I'll…I'll leave you to it."

She hurried away and he returned to his suitcase, trying to recall what it was the Dupres had wanted him to do anyway. He found his notebook tucked into the pocket on the lid and checked what he'd discussed with Milton. Something for pollinators, something to keep away diseases and to nourish the soil; standard upkeep.

He fished out what he needed and loaded the jars into his pockets. They clinked together as he walked outside and he almost lost a few when he stooped to shed his boots and socks. This sort of thing was really done best with no clothes at all, but it was cold and he didn't think the Dupres would care for the display.

He cuffed his jeans and buried his toes in the dirt, feeling a little warmer and safer than he had a moment ago. Touching the earth always brought him closer to home.

Or, he corrected, closer to the place that had been home. He couldn't go back, not yet, and probably not ever. The Devil had vowed that he would bring them back, but June doubted that going back to Heaven would ever be the same as going home again.

He closed his eyes, pushing away those thoughts, and opened himself up, letting in the smell of rain and the sound of birds and rustle of branches. He heard, far off, voices of the Dupres and the thin, high voice of Prudence battering James Kelly with questions about the difference between Africans and Negros.

June took out the first jar he needed and headed off into the trees, down each row, chanting under his breath and laying down spells to feed the earth. He sprinkled powder from the jar as he went and when he was done, he took care to wash his hands thoroughly, lest he chew his nails and ingest some of the powder.

It wouldn't kill him but it wouldn't be pleasant either, considering that he wasn't a tree.

He walked the land three times in total, stopping a few times for a drink of water; the constant chanting and spell-working dried his throat. Sending out his power like this wore him out and he thought he would ask Dolly for a cup of coffee if she didn't mind.

It was a good kind of tired, though, a tired that came from working hard and helping. The trees reached out to him just as much as he reached for them. He could feel each rainfall, each dry spell, all the apples they had grown and each blossom that had never born fruit. He knew each branch that needed trimming and which ones had been pruned back too hard.

Bees would be coming out from their cocoons soon, ready to mate and build their nests. Butterflies would be along when the weather had warmed enough. In the woods some miles east, a bear and her cub slept. Part of him wanted to stay out here forever, build a little cabin in the wood where he'd always be able to smell good, green things.

No matter how many green things he crammed into his apartment, it would never be enough.

He stood at the edge of the orchard, facing out towards the forest, recalling times when he had been lost. Years in the Hanging Gardens came to mind first; the memories would remain vague unless he really tried to remember. Now wasn't the time for that, he had a schedule to keep and didn't need to end up wandering the forest. He thought of the trek between Georgia and Pennsylvania when he'd been little more than a fleeing animal, foraging for food and sleeping in trees.

He brought himself out of that after a while and willed himself back to the farmhouse, dragged mostly by the thought of coffee and the promise of sharing a real bed with James Kelly that night.

Edna found him while he was rinsing off his feet with the hose, shivering and wanting to bury himself in the earth so he could be warm again. She hovered off to the side and when he finally realized she was there, it was only because he'd been startled by a glimpse of her skirt out of the corner of his eye.

He turned to look at her and recalled that she'd asked him for help with something. "Edna."

"It's...do you think you'd have time?"

He nodded.

She gestured for him to follow her inside and he went, still barefoot. He trailed her upstairs, guilty over the wet, but clean, footprints that he left behind.

"I have something to show you," she told him, opening the door to her bedroom.

He had the vague idea that he should tell her that he wasn't single, but forgot about that immediately when the overwhelming chill in the room struck him. She had her windows wide open.

He pushed his hands inside his jacket pockets, wishing he'd put his boots on.

While he thought about warmer things, she went over to the window and pulled in something off the roof.

She approached him carrying a wooden box, the kind with a latch and lock. Love letters and mementos, he would have guessed, and he opened his mouth to tell her that he didn't do love spells. She unlocked the box with a key she wore around her neck. All his words dried up when she lifted the lid and turned it towards him.

Nestled inside the box and swaddled in a bit of pink fabric lay a baby.

No.

Not a baby, it hadn't gotten the chance to be a baby. The thing would have fit in the palm of his hand.

It had died a long time ago. A month, at least. He couldn't tell exactly because the poor thing had been frozen. Kept out on the roof in that box, maybe all winter.

Edna moved closer to him. "I...I kept him safe, you know, but the weather, it's going to get warm soon. I couldn't stand to think of him in the freezer! Can you bring him back?"

Put him back inside me. The words hung unspoken between them. He thought he might be sick.

"Bury it."

She recoiled physically, drawing the box closer to her chest. "You said you could help."

He shook his head. He thought she'd wanted something easy. "No. Not for this. Not..."

"You're a *demon*."

"Not that sort," he said but couldn't think of a single demon he knew that would do what she'd asked. Even the Devil himself would have advised the girl to dig a grave. Dead things weren't meant to come back and never after so long.

"You've got to help," she insisted, tears and snot streaking down her face. She took in a long shaking breath. "He's all I've got."

He shook his head, backing away. He tried to swallow the lump in his throat, a choking combination of bile and mucus. "Bury it, it's all you can do."

"There's got to be something else!"

"There's nothing. Your baby's dead, Edna, I'm so sorry—"

"What do you know about sorry!" she screamed.

"Bury him, put him in the earth so he can be something good," he insisted. "Let him rest."

She shook her head. "No."

He moved towards her. "I can help with that much."

"Don't!" She retreated, backed herself up against the wall, clutching the box to her chest as though it were a living child and he meant to drag it from her. She slid down the wall, pulling up her knees, her whole body curled around the box. "Don't."

"It's the only thing to be done."

She began to sob and he put his hand on her shoulder. She didn't seem to notice at all, but she resisted when he tried to take the box from her.

Crouching beside her like this, still holding on to the box, he felt intrusive. He didn't want to be anywhere near her or this dead thing. "What's his name?"

"Franklin."

"Alright. Hand him to me."

"No."

"Edna, please. You had to know."

"He's all I've got left."

"That's not true. You've got a whole life left. You'll have other babies and you'll love them just as much. I promise." He pulled gently on the box.

He thought she would refuse again but her grasp loosened. It didn't have anything to do with his poor attempts at comfort; grief had run her ragged and she couldn't keep her grip on the box any longer. "Put him somewhere he can see the stars."

"I will," he promised. He took the box from her before she could change her mind.

He passed by James Kelly and Prudence on the porch as he walked out. The vampire called to him, but June couldn't stop. If he stopped, he would come undone.

He walked out past the orchard and into the woods.

He'd lied to Edna. He didn't bury her baby in view of the stars. Dead things couldn't see. She would never need to know. He dug down as deep as he could until his fingers cramped and his nails started to crack.

He lifted the tiny corpse from the box and nestled it into the earth. He said the only prayer he'd ever had for the dead, a prayer for rest, a prayer that this body would give life to something else.

He built a small cairn and made his way back to the car.

James Kelly approached him as he left the woods, his shoulders hunched and his face drawn tight. "They, uh, they've asked us to leave."

June nodded.

"It's...well, it's not you, you know, they don't hold anything against you, at least that's what they said. That man, whatever his name was, he said something about having family matters to take care of. Listen, I'm not clear what's going on, but that girl is upset about something," the vampire rambled. "June?"

He didn't have anything to say.

"Listen. Uh. She'd said something about a baby."

He nodded.

"Oh. Well. Anyway. I've packed up the car."

"Thanks."

James Kelly followed him to the car and watched anxiously as he pulled on his socks and boots.

He backed down the driveway faster than he should have, wanting nothing more than to be away from this place. He very nearly got them killed when he swung out on to the road.

"June!" James Kelly cried.

He ignored him, trying to correct the car. He barreled down the road, not able to do anything but flee.

"Pull over."

He didn't.

"Pull over!" the vampire barked.

The shout sent a jolt through June. They'd argued before and James Kelly had raised his voice with him before, but never like that. It turned his insides to jelly, but he obeyed, crookedly parking the Rambler on the side of the road.

"Shit!" James Kelly declared. "What's the idea, huh?"

"I'm sorry," June whispered.

Anger oozed off the vampire's face but June didn't feel any better. James Kelly reached towards him and June shrank back.

"I'm sorry but you were going to get us killed!"

"I know."

"What's got you so shaken up?"

He shook his head and started to cry. He didn't have any

words let alone the right ones.

James Kelly slid over closer to him and put a hand on his shoulder. "June, come on. What happened?"

He couldn't answer. All he could do was blubber and he knew how much James Kelly didn't like tears. "I'm sorry." He tried to wipe his eyes but his hands were dirty, which only made it so he was upset and had dirt in his eyes.

"Stop touching your eyes," James Kelly told him but he couldn't stop. The vampire grabbed him by the wrists and pulled his hands away from his face. "God, you're going to hurt yourself. Come here, let me see."

James Kelly cupped his hands around June's face and examined June's eyes as he fought his tears, his breath coming in little hitches. June reached up again and James Kelly pushed his hands back down. "Stop." He used a handkerchief to dab around June's eyes, clearing away the dirt.

"I'm so sorry."

"Stop apologizing. Why are you crying?"

"Because I'm sad."

James Kelly sighed. "No, I mean...June, it's not because I shouted, is it? I didn't...you needed to pull over."

His mouth sticky and his nose running, he answered, "No."

"Then what?"

He shook his head. It was too much and he didn't have the right words to explain any of it. "I don't know. I don't. I'm sorry." His crying returned with renewed strength.

James Kelly seemed to realize he was fighting a losing battle trying to get an answer out of him, so he pulled June into his arms. "Well, whatever it is you might as well cry yourself out at this point."

"I'm sorry."

"Stop apologizing."

"I—"

The vampire tightened his arms. "Shush."

June shushed, partially because James Kelly had squeezed all the air out of his lungs. The vampire relaxed his embrace after a moment and June could continue his weeping unrestricted. It wasn't a cathartic cry where he felt clean and calm afterward, but one that left him tired and sort of feeling like he should jump off a building.

When he stopped, James Kelly pulled back and smoothed June's hair back. He handed him the handkerchief and smiled when June blew his nose. It was a rare but not totally unfamiliar smile, straddling a line between tenderness, pity, and amusement. James Kelly smiled like that when the cat fell into the shower by accident or when Mrs. Grabowska got lost on their floor. *You sweet, dumb thing*, said the smile, *What a poor fool you are.*

"Why don't you let me drive?" James Kelly asked the same way he told Mrs. Grabowska, "Why don't you let me walk you upstairs?"

June nodded and as he reached for the handle, James Kelly grabbed him by the arm and asked, "You're alright, aren't you?"

"I don't know."

James Kelly made a face, his lips pressed together and quirked off to one side like he was thinking hard. He let go of June and they switched sides.

James Kelly didn't seem to have any trouble finding a place for them to lodge for the night; he pulled over only once for a brief consultation with a roadmap and the *Green Book*. June had worried about where they would stay for the whole drive between the Dupre orchard and the motel the vampire had found. He worried when James Kelly went into the office, too, but the other man came out not ten minutes later with a key in his hand and a smile on his face.

June tried to smile back but couldn't manage much.

Once he'd lugged his suitcase inside, he moved towards the bed, intending to collapse on it and sleep for about a thousand years. James Kelly caught him around the waist before he could and brought him into an embrace. It took June by surprise and, coupled with everything else, brought him back to the verge of tears.

He lay his head against James Kelly's shoulder, careful not to scrape, poke, or otherwise injure him with his horns.

"Wash up, why don't you?" the vampire suggested mildly.

He was right, of course; not too long into the drive, June had needed to take off his socks and brush off his feet to get rid of all the twigs and leaves that he'd brought out of the forest with him. He still had dirt beneath his claws and caked into the cracks.

After he'd cleaned up, he sank into the bed, though. James Kelly sat beside him and June wondered if they'd sleep apart tonight. He'd booked a room with two beds.

Posterity, June assured himself.

James Kelly examined one of June's claws. "Is it..."

"Hmm?"

"Doesn't that hurt?"

June looked over to see that he was talking about the split running down one of his claws. It did hurt, a dull, underlying throb. In total, he counted two splits, one of which he expected to fall off, and three with broken points. The jagged points he would have to trim or file, otherwise, he'd be scratching people and snagging fabric left and right. "Not really."

The vampire made a face, which compelled June to go back into the bathroom and search through his toiletries for nail clippers.

He found them and trimmed his claws, a process that was incredibly uncomfortable. His nails were not thin and plaint like most people's and trimming them always ran the risk of injury. He even clipped the split oncs as best he could so they would be even.

Afterward, he stared down at his fingers, which now seemed stunted and uneven. The shape of his nails when pared and filed always seemed blunt and ugly to him.

Claws had a thousand and one uses, everything from scratching a someone's back to being able to write in wax and clay tablets without a stylus, though that hadn't come in handy for some years now.

Of course, they had their drawbacks, too. He had to be careful when it came to certain types of sex, otherwise, someone was likely to get hurt. Not that he wasn't good at being careful.

He returned to bed, burying his face in the pillow and wondered if he should extend the offer to James Kelly. "Only time I can put my fingers inside you without running the risk of shredding your insides. Better take it while you can," he could have said. He imagined the flushed and wide-eyed shock the offer would have produced.

June didn't think James Kelly knew any of the details about how two men would go about having sex with each other. The concept sounded straightforward but nothing was ever as easy as it sounded.

They had time, though, to get to things like that. Lots of time,

June hoped. He watched James Kelly move around the room, unpacking a few things.

"You know, they've got a pool. Closed for the season, obviously!" the vampire said, "But I haven't been for a swim in ages."

June thought about what James Kelly would look like at the beach, gloriously brown and glowing in the sunlight, so much of his skin exposed in swim shorts. It was a miracle that more men didn't go after each other when they wore little shorts like that. Beaches were nothing but toned thighs and smooth shoulders and flat stomachs, young men laughing and hanging off of each other.

He would like to see James Kelly at the beach, June decided.

It was the last thing he thought for a while, sliding into hazy dreams.

He didn't know how much later it was when James Kelly shook him awake, a gentle hand on his back and the smell of meatloaf.

He pushed himself and rubbed his eyes, wondering why on earth the vampire who refused to eat would smell like food.

"You shouldn't go to the beach," June told him, not able to think clearly and preoccupied with the tight, stubby feeling of his fingers.

"No?"

"Too much sun. You'll probably get hives or something." Vampires could go out in the sun, of course, but too much direct sunlight tended to have adverse effects, depending on the vampire. Some of them reacted terribly and ended up flaking and peeling for days.

"Night swimming, then," James Kelly told him. "I brought you something to eat."

"Meatloaf." The smell made sense now.

"Yes. Come on, sit up."

June sat up all the way and went over to the small table that James Kelly had nodded towards. "Did you eat?" he asked.

"No."

"You know what I meant."

"I'm alright."

June frowned.

"I am, I swear. I'd...I'd say something if I wasn't. I don't want, well, you know, I don't want any slip-ups."

June nodded. He undid the takeout container and stared at the meatloaf, an unsettling combination of hungry and nauseated. It wasn't the meatloaf, it was that he hadn't eaten in hours. He would feel better when he'd eaten; he told himself this over and over until he was able to stop staring and take a bite.

James Kelly sat across from him while he ate, smoking and doing the crossword puzzle in an old newspaper that he must have scrounged up somewhere.

"We'll get you a real paper in the morning," June promised, "And postcards."

"Sure."

June checked his watch and was floored, in a vague and distant way, to realize that he had only spent one night away from home. That he hadn't even spent a full day away from Sissy. Something about seeing that small, frozen body had warped his world.

"You look terrible."

June's head jerked up.

"I meant to say that you should finish eating and get some rest."

"Mmm."

June managed to ingest about half the food and had to throw the rest away, not able to look at it anymore. He thought James Kelly would be offended and ask him, "Don't you *like* meatloaf?" in that prickly, affronted tone he got when he thought he had done something wrong.

Instead, though, he gave June's shoulder a squeeze and told him, "You'll feel better once you've had a real night's sleep. Can't imagine that couch did you any good, either."

Sleep didn't come easily; he'd turned in early, before the clock even showed nine o'clock. James Kelly had pulled up the covers for him then retreated to one corner, sitting beside a small lamp, scratching away at the crossword puzzle.

June watched him, eyes half closed. "You stuck on one?"

James Kelly glanced over. "Thought you were asleep."

"Can't."

"Should I turn the light off?"

"What word are you stuck on?"

"Five letter word, starts with s. A grass-like plant that prefers wet ground."

June counted the letters on his fingers, then said, "Sedge."

"You would know that, wouldn't you?"

He didn't know what to say to that.

"You really should get some rest."

Not wanting to, feeling pathetic and desperate, June mumbled, "Will you come lay down with me?"

James Kelly nodded, left behind his paper and pen, and came over to the bed, shedding his clothes first, down to his underclothes. He left everything neatly hung or folded, except for what could not be worn again.

He slid right under the covers beside June, folding June into his arms. He leaned in from behind and nuzzled his cheek against June's. "You smell nice." He settled in against June's back and kissed his shoulder. "Love you."

"I'm sorry I was such a mess before."

For no more than ten seconds, James Kelly was quiet but it was long enough to make June think he'd said something wrong. "You haven't got to apologize."

"I know you don't like it when people cry."

"I...June." James Kelly sighed. He butted his forehead against June's shoulder. "You go on and cry if you've got to, never mind how I feel about it."

"But if you—"

"Shh. Really. Go to sleep."

June tried, he did. He wanted to sleep but suddenly all he could think of was baseball. "Wei likes baseball, too, you know. And Andrew's wild for it. We should go to a game."

"I don't think Wei likes me much."

"No, he doesn't, but he likes me."

After a beat, James Kelly inquired, "He's a funny sort, though, isn't he? The way he talks..."

"He's from England."

"I know that! Just...it's a hell of an accent."

"It's...well, it's not fake, you know, but it's...exaggerated. He didn't speak a lick of English until he was eight or so. His mom only spoke Chinese to him so when he started to learn, everyone used to give him a real hard time about his accent. You know, the Chinese accent. So he covered it up."

"Oh."

June could tell from the quality of the silence that the vampire felt bad for having said anything at all.

"I like his real accent better, I tell him all the time. You have to get him *incredibly* drunk...or angry! But you didn't hear it from me."

"Course not."

"You ever see *The Pygmalion?*"

"No."

"With Leslie Howard?"

"I already said no."

With a giddy chuckle, June suggested, "Call him Eliza Doolittle sometime and see how mad he gets!"

"I figure I probably won't."

June shook his head and told him, "You will, you'll hold on to it until he crosses you. You're like that, you know, you hold on to things till you need them. Till it'll sting the most."

James Kelly didn't pull away but something about the way he was holding June changed. His arms loosened and he wasn't nestled quite as close. He didn't say anything else and June didn't either; he didn't know what to say. The words had slipped out and June knew they were harsh, but he also knew they were true.

The morning of the twelfth found June in bed alone, huddled beneath two blankets to keep out the early morning chill. James Kelly must have fetched the second blanket from the other bed because June didn't remember getting it himself.

The ashtray in front of the vampire said he'd smoked about half a dozen cigarettes so far that morning. He wasn't usually an early riser and June still didn't know if that was by nature or left over from seven years thinking he couldn't go out into the sun.

June pushed himself up and rubbed the sand from his eyes. "Morning."

"Morning."

"Shower?"

"I did already."

June hoped his disappointment didn't show too clearly. He should have noticed that James Kelly was already dressed, anyway, and known better than to ask.

By the time he had finished in the shower, James Kelly had packed up all their things, leaving a change of clothes out on the bed for June.

It struck June as oddly maternal, though he didn't think any mother would ever lay out blue jeans, a leather jacket, and a black t-shirt for their son, no matter how wayward he was.

He toweled off his hair, surveying the clothes. "Do you think I look a fool?"

"You aren't wearing any pants," James Kelly answered helpfully.

"No! I mean. Dressing like that." He jutted his chin towards his clothes.

"Like a greaser? No. I don't think so."

"No?"

"No," he confirmed.

June shimmied into the clothes. "The music is something, though."

"You better be careful listening to that race music," James Kelly said severely, in his flattest, whitest voice. "You never know what those Negros are up to these days."

June snorted.

In his usual cadence, James Kelly added, "Anyway, we both know you're just trying to look like Marlon Brando."

"I'll have you know I traded for this jacket before *The Wild One* even played in theaters."

"Even before you saw the posters for it?" James Kelly asked.

"Yes!" June insisted.

James Kelly raised an eyebrow.

"You'll just have to admit someday that I'm hip."

The vampire pressed a hand to his mouth and June thought it might have been to hide a smile, so he persisted, saying, "I am just about fluent in jive talk, you know, I've been around the scene for a while. Some of the cats down at the club say I'm cool, they'll invite me back up to their crib for a bit of reefer after the gig."

James Kelly let out a harsh snort.

"Hey, man, don't blow your lid! That grass is alright!"

Through his suppressed laugh, James Kelly choked out, "Stop."

June had gotten the laugh he'd wanted but felt the need to explain, "I was seeing this fellow in Harlem for a little while. Well. I mean. For a little while at a time. On and off for a few years."

"Did you?" James Kelly seemed more interested and less amused now.

He shrugged on his jacket. "Sure. The Navy gave him a blue ticket and sent him back home. Hung around in a lot of jazz clubs. He didn't play anything, though, he was the tea-man. Which is not a bad type of fellow to be seeing."

"In Harlem."

"What, do you think there's a neighborhood in Manhattan I haven't set foot in?" he asked. "I am the Watcher."

James Kelly nodded.

"I could use a bite to eat," June announced when neither of them had spoken for a little too long.

James Kelly took up his suitcase and headed for the door.

Before he could open it, though, June caught up to him and put a hand on the door and gave what he hoped was a meaningful look, expectant but not desperate. He was not in the mood for much, but it felt wrong to head back into the world without a kiss.

James Kelly hesitated, his eyes sliding towards the shades to make sure they were drawn, but he set down his suitcase then he leaned in. He kissed June several times but did not restrict himself to June's lips, his mouth crawling down to press against June's throat.

June tensed, his heart fluttering a little because James Kelly had pushed him up against the door and opened his mouth against June's throat. A bite was coming, he was sure, he just couldn't tell if it would be a frisky nip or one with intent to draw blood. Some vampires, he knew, could have a hard time telling the difference. So far, James Kelly had been reliable about not breaking skin.

The vampire pulled back when June tensed, but June slid one hand around the back of his head, urging him in for one last kiss. If he took any more than that he didn't think he'd be able to let their bodies separate any time soon.

He let him go after he'd gotten the kiss and they left the motel room like they were nothing more than business partners.

June amused himself contemplating what it would be like for

James Kelly to be in the fertility business. He even voiced the idea to the other man when they were about half way between Rochester and Syracuse as they made their way south towards the Finger Lakes.

James Kelly looked up from the map and asked, "Weren't you supposed to take that exit?"

"No."

"Are you sure?" he asked in a voice that suggested June should not be sure at all.

"I've driven this route about six thousand times—"

"Don't get hyperbolic."

"Hyperbolic! Shit, if you do any more crossword puzzles I'm not going to be able to follow a thing you're saying."

James Kelly scowled.

"I know where I'm going, don't worry. Right outside of Seneca Lake. Dairy farm. You like cows?"

"Never had an occasion to meet one."

"I think you will."

"Meet one? Probably, it's a dairy farm," the vampire reasoned.

June glanced over and James Kelly looked back, perfectly serious. "Uh."

The other man raised his eyebrows, expectant.

"Never mind." June couldn't tell if he was being sincere or not.

A hint of a smile flickered over James Kelly's face. He placed a hand on June's thigh, not high enough up to be frisky, and squeezed gently.

After another half an hour, James Kelly had turned to lean against the car door, one leg dangling to the side and the other pulled up to rest against the back of the seat. It was a casual, relaxed pose that June liked on him.

He gazed in June's direction, but June knew he was looking out the window. He knew because he was attempting to play 'I spy'. "I see something—"

"It better not be another goddamned tree."

"Red."

June glanced up and down the road. He saw no red cars.

"It's in the car."

June frowned and tried to evaluate the car as best he could

without sending them careening off the road. "I don't know."

"It's small."

June looked towards him, a little irritated and intending to tell him off, but ended up saying, "Your tie."

"Yes! Your turn."

"You know I really don't—"

"I can't read in the car," James Kelly admitted.

"You get car sick or something?"

"No. Not really."

"Then what?"

The vampire shrugged. "I don't know, I get distracted."

"By all the nothing going on around us?" June asked. James Kelly didn't answer so after about a minute June said, "Fine. I see something..." He sighed. "Blue?"

"The sky."

"No."

"You."

"No."

"Give me another clue."

"It smells."

"You," James Kelly said again.

"Hey!"

"The air freshener."

"Yes."

The vampire rolled his shoulders. "If you don't want to play 'I spy' what do you want to do?"

"I don't know. Think of something to talk about. What are you going to write to your parents?"

They had stopped that morning for cigarettes and gotten postcards as well.

"I don't know."

June recognized the sulky tone in his voice right away. "What's that pout for?"

"I'm not pouting."

"And, by the way, are you ever going to start speaking with your parents again? Your mother calls an awful lot."

"I don't know what to say to her now," the other man confessed.

"I never had a mother of my own, but I do know that from their offspring parents generally like to hear that everything is well."

"You don't have a mother?"

"Don't change the topic, you know I haven't got a mother," June admonished. "Why are you avoiding your parents?"

"Because."

"You took me to meet them," June began carefully. "It didn't seem to go so bad."

James Kelly sighed and June thought that was all he'd get out of him, but he ran hands over his face and through his hair, then said, "No."

"No, it didn't go so bad or...?"

"No, it didn't go so bad," he confirmed. "Better than it should have."

"But?"

"But they thought I was dead."

June glanced his way. "Uh. I'm not sure I follow, sweetheart."

James Kelly raised his eyebrows and June thought he would protest the term of endearment, but he instead explained, "They thought I was dead and when I was with Annie I was just about as good as dead to them anyway. I barely visited and when I did, I was either coming right off a kill or starving for another one."

June made eye contact, then returned his eyes to the road. "Go ahead."

"So now I'm not dead and I'm not killing people—God! Not that I ever told them I was. But I'm. You know, I'm more or less normal. And I know it was killing them when I wasn't. I could just...the way my mother would watch me like she didn't know who I was. And she was right. I wasn't...I wasn't really *me* like that. With Annie."

"Sure."

"I'm, you know, I'm me again. And she thinks that means that I can go back to an ordinary life. They both do. They think I can pick up the life I was supposed to have again."

"And what's that mean?" June asked, genuinely curious. He'd never had a life that could be considered ordinary by any stretch of the imagination.

"It means I settle down and have kids. It means I find a job being a clerk or a janitor and I go home and...and my wife's got dinner on the table but...You know, I died and my parents, they're not going to do anything that's going to, to get rid of me. So if I'm shacked up with some man, they're not going to say anything about it. Not directly."

"But?"

"But my mother is going to try to set me up with any girl she can find. And my father is going to...June, the way he looks at me! I know he wants to say something. I know all the things he's thinking."

June waited, the silence long and heavy.

"I heard the jokes, you know, the ones they all make about the guy at work who everyone knows is a queer. The impressions they do, the comments and the...all of it. And maybe my parents weren't always the ones making the comments, but they laughed. They never invited those people over for parties. I *know* he wants to say something. I know they're disappointed. I know if things hadn't fallen the way they had, then I'd be someone they didn't invite over. That you'd be someone they'd make fun of."

June let that sit for a while, not sure how he felt. "I...uh. Everyone does sort of peg me for a queer right away."

James Kelly cleared his throat.

"I don't...I don't know how they know but everyone does," June confessed.

Harold and Elizabeth had let him into their home, they'd broken bread together. He'd washed their dishes and, like the idiot he was, he'd believed that indicated some degree of acceptance. He'd never expected it to be whole-hearted. At least, not as anything more than a pipe dream.

"I can't be quiet about it. Even when I try."

"I know," James Kelly told him. The statement came with a heaviness to it, as though James Kelly had long accepted that even being seen with June was going to put him under suspicion. "Pull over, will you?"

June pulled over. He expected James Kelly to get out of the car, maybe even ask June to turn around and bring him to a train station or something. Ask for the key so he could get his stuff and be gone by the time June had finished his trip.

Instead, he crossed the distance between them and put his arms around June. He held on tight and June couldn't shake the feeling that it was a farewell embrace. A sharp twinge shot through him; he didn't want to go back to how things had been.

He was simply not the sort of man that inspired long-term relationships. Rarely had anyone ever wanted him for as long as he had wanted them. He had never been the one to walk away.

James Kelly didn't say anything; he didn't get out or ask to be taken somewhere else, though June would have brought him anywhere he wanted to go. He pulled in steady, calm breaths and kept his arms around June.

June curled himself into James Kelly's embrace. "I'm sorry."

"For what?" He pulled back, brow creased.

"Everything. I shouldn't...I shouldn't have gotten you into this. Shouldn't have gone asking you about things when I *knew* you didn't want to talk about them."

"Don't."

June pressed on. "It's true, though, I, you know, I've only *got* one way to be, but *you*, you know, you could...go and keep on being with women. But I...I kept at it. Trying to get you to talk about it. And now..."

"Do you remember when you came to get me? When I called you because Annie had brought someone home?"

June remembered. Anastasia had brought home a willing victim, a woman who'd wanted to die. June had found James Kelly locked onto that woman, dangerously close to taking another life.

"And I told you off when we got outside, right? Cause I thought you were going to kiss me."

"I was only going to ask," June vowed. Ask and pray that James Kelly would say yes.

"I spent...God, I must have thought about it every day from then until New Year's. That was it, really, that was when I really knew...cause every day I was...wishing I'd let you, wishing I'd never met you, wishing I could stop thinking about everything so much. Wishing I could let myself have what I wanted."

"Oh." June hadn't known that. He couldn't have, of course, but he wished he had.

"So I can't. I can't go find some woman and take up with her because she won't be you. No one else, not a man or a woman, will ever be you."

"Oh." June was sure he had something else to say; he could even feel the thoughts hazily floating through his mind, some loving and profound confession of his own, but 'oh' was the only thing he could grasp.

"Okay?" James Kelly asked, sliding his palm against June's cheek.

June burrowed against his hand, catching the other man's hand between his face and his shoulder, wishing he knew how to feel or what to do. He had never ruined someone's life before and didn't know how to feel now that it seemed James Kelly was complicit in his own destruction.

"You're not ruining my life."

June didn't know how the vampire had read his mind.

"You asked me before if you were. If I wanted you to be a woman. You're not. And I don't."

"Thanks for clearing it up."

James Kelly leaned in and touched his forehead to June's. They stayed like that, nose to nose, eyes shut, until James Kelly gave him a kiss. "I love you. I think about that every day now instead."

At first, June didn't know how to feel but good feelings started to bubble up, filling his chest and making him grin. "I love you, too."

MARCH 16, 1954.

A flat tire should not have confounded a demon who had fought by the Devil's side and lived through millennia since the Fall. In fact, it hadn't before. This flat tire, however, was different. He'd gotten the jack and the tire iron from the trunk, taken out the spare, and removed the flat. He'd even put the spare onto the car. Now he stood with the iron in his hand, looking at the flat tire.

"We're gonna be late," he told the car.

James Kelly lit a cigarette and glanced up at the sky. Stars speckled the expanse and the moon would be full in a few days. "You'd better finish up then."

It had gotten dark between when June had started and when he'd looked down for the lug nuts. "I, well."

"What?" James Kelly asked.

"I can't."

"Why not?"

"I lost the lug nuts."

The vampire straightened up, looked around on the ground, then pronounced, "That is a problem, huh?"

"You don't see them?"

"No."

June stepped carefully away from the car. He squinted into the grass but didn't see a gleam or glimmer, not even in the light provided by the moon and stars. Generally, the Fallen and vampires had decent vision in low light.

James Kelly peered around a little more. "Did you kick them or something?"

"I don't think so. I don't remember it."

The vampire let out a low growl.

They hadn't seen much of civilization for the past couple of days. Their plan for that night had been to stop in a fairly well-populated town so that James Kelly could find a donor. June had tried to get him to do it earlier, but he'd balked at the only donor they'd been able to find.

She had been young, maybe twenty, and wan, with dark circles under her eyes. She had been the only one in the small town willing to suffer a vampire's bite, but James Kelly had hesitated, saying that a bite was likely to do her harm.

She'd insisted that she'd be fine and had offered to take less than they'd offered.

At first, June had thought she might be one of the rare types of junkies that chased vampires but when she'd offered to do a variety of other things for James Kelly at similarly low prices, he'd realized that she was simply desperate for money.

James Kelly had given her five dollars and walked away.

June hadn't like the idea of stretching him thin like this, but James Kelly had insisted that he was fine. He hadn't wanted to hear June's offer either.

"You..." June began.

The vampire turned towards him.

"There's a flashlight. I'll look around. You can wait in the car."

James Kelly didn't get into the car. He glowered and smoked while June carefully combed the road and grass for the lug nuts. He couldn't find them anywhere, not after an hour of searching.

"Maybe someone will drive by," he offered hopefully when he felt that looking any longer would be pointless.

"Maybe," James Kelly agreed, his voice flat and strained.

June looked towards the river to their right. They'd left the Finger Lakes, where they'd visited two dairy farms, and had been headed northwest towards the last apple orchard. Their last stop before the festival in the Adirondacks.

They'd been making good time, too, and even losing a day of travel wouldn't do their itinerary any harm.

They'd only be late for getting James Kelly someone to bite.

"Maybe we'll be able to see them in the morning."

The vampire ground out the butt of his cigarette. "Morning?"

"Or I figure one of us could walk, try to get to town, maybe. Though I don't figure people are selling lug nuts at this hour," June said.

"Things don't *just* disappear."

June wanted to say that no, they didn't, but sometimes they got taken. He looked again at the river and the oak tree on its bank. He swallowed. "Well, uh. I can keep looking."

James Kelly glared, but then his face softened. He put away his pack of cigarettes and said, "I'm sorry."

"Oh."

"Snapping at you isn't going to fix anything. I'm sorry."

June nodded.

James Kelly had been doing that more. Catching himself when he was being irritable, apologizing before June had to remind him that he was being hurtful. He moved in closer to June and put an arm around his shoulder, pulling him in close. "I can look for a bit."

June handed him the flashlight but even after another hour, he had no better luck that June.

No cars had driven by, either, and June didn't think any would for a while yet. He hunched his shoulders and pulled his jacket more tightly around himself. He wished he'd packed warmer socks.

James Kelly went further in his search than June had, over towards the river. He looked under the tree, then paused for a while, staring at the river.

June approached him, wondering if he'd spotted them glimmering on the riverbed. "What?"

"No, I...Nothing."

"Maybe you can get some sleep."

"Hmm?"

"And I've got a whole pack of cigarettes. It should help keep the edge off. I'm sure we'll be able to find someone—"

"I'm fine."

"I don't think you are," June ventured. He'd noted a slight pallor and sheen to the vampire's skin, though he hadn't started to shake yet and that was good. The thirstier he was, the more difficult it would be for him to control himself. "I think. Well. We talked about it, you know, and I *have* offered."

The vampire's eyes darted towards June, quick and sharp, before he stepped away. "I can wait."

"I don't want you to."

"We're in the middle of nowhere."

June didn't understand what that could have to do with it. If anything, it was better to do this away from humans and prying eyes. "So?"

"So no one...no one would be able to help you." He looked at the ground. "If I, if I can't stop."

"I trust you."

"I don't know how to make it good," James Kelly warned him, "Like the ones the junkies chase."

June shrugged. "It's up to you. I'm not trying to force you into anything."

The vampire nodded, though he didn't appear to be agreeing to take June's blood.

"You want to at least go neck in the car?"

His gaze flicked towards the road and June expected him to decline. He expected him to pace around all night smoking while June watched, useless and fretting. James Kelly took a step towards the car, his hand dipping into his pocket to find his cigarettes.

He changed direction without warning and it was one of the few times that June was reminded that he was a vampire in the complete sense. He came towards June, his movement smooth and easy, and his hands gripped June's waist. He had June backed up against the tree so quick that June wasn't quite sure what he was doing, not until he pushed one leg between June's and drew him into a deep kiss.

His skin started to grow hot and James Kelly's hands slipped inside June's jacket, peeling him out of it. One hand held June's bare arm, a thumb pressing into his wrist; June could feel his heart hammering, especially there, the vein thrumming against his grip.

His face burned and against the chill of the night air, June felt aflame, he had the sense that if James Kelly let him go he would burn up and float away like a scrap of paper escaping from a blaze.

"Tell me if I should stop."

June nodded, mute, his lips aching for another kiss, but James Kelly didn't kiss him again. He sank to his knees, still holding June's arm, and pressed his mouth to the crook of his elbow.

June whimpered when his teeth broke skin, but James Kelly didn't notice, or if he noticed, he didn't care. Instead, he pulled steadily, his mouth locked onto June's arm. The wound throbbed as he pulled, a strange feeling that June almost didn't like until he caught the low, pleased sigh that the vampire let out.

That sound sent another roll of heat through June and it doubled when the vampire's free hand kneaded his leg, climbing up his thigh.

And then James Kelly's mouth was no longer on his arm but pressed to his stomach, and his hands were unzipping his jeans, pulling them lower, slowly. James Kelly glanced up, licked his lips, and asked, "You don't mind?"

A sound that was almost laughter escaped June. "No."

June didn't mind at all, not the roughness of the bark at his back or the smell of damp soil around them. He didn't mind that James Kelly's fangs scraped against him the smallest bit as he took June into his mouth, just as fevered as he had been taking June's blood. He forgot about the aching bite on his arm, thinking only of this. Every worry he'd had about the two of them was gone, replaced with the immediacy of being together and being whole and loved.

James Kelly dug his fingers into June's thigh when he spilled, letting out a bit of a grunt that at first June thought must have been one of displeasure until he took June in a little deeper and swallowed.

When he moved away, June sank down into his arms and buried his face in his neck. The vampire nuzzled into his shoulder, then wrapped his arms around June and squeezed hard.

June squeaked, all the air pushed out of his lungs, and wheezed, "Christ, you're strong."

James Kelly loosened his grip. "Sorry."

He brushed his fingers across the other man's cheek, then panicked briefly when he left a trail of tacky blood across his skin.

James Kelly reached up, touching the blood. "I..." He reached into his jacket and pulled out a handkerchief, pressing it to the bite on June's arm. "I'm sorry...I should have..."

"I'm not complaining."

"Still."

June kissed him. "Even a little." He licked his thumb and scrubbed the blood from James Kelly's cheek.

He stood, holding the handkerchief to his arm, and tucked himself back into his clothes with his other hand. He approached the river and knelt at the bank, having given up on keeping these jeans clean when he'd noticed a smear of blood down one leg.

He rinsed the blood from his arm, wincing at the chill of the water and looked back at James Kelly, who still knelt in by the tree.

"We'll find a laundromat," June told him as he secured the handkerchief around his forearm.

His fingers played over his lips and he pulled his hand away when June addressed him. "What?"

"In that town. We'll take a day, get everything washed up, you know. We've got a little time to spare. You can finally fill out that postcard."

"What am I supposed to write?"

"What people always write on trips. Having a wonderful time, seeing all the sights, the missus says hi, see you when we get back." June moved back towards him, pushing his hands into the pockets of his jeans.

James Kelly stood, brushing off his trousers. "I told my mother I'd go for dinner. She says Patty Gleeson just moved back from Chicago, thinks we should catch up."

"Well, if you told her you'd go."

"She thinks we'd get along." James Kelly picked up June's jacket and held it so he could slip into it.

June let the vampire help him into his jacket, feeling especially tickled by the gesture. "You might."

"June!"

"What? I'm not saying make love to her on the kitchen table! But, you know, you can go and be polite."

James Kelly snorted and shook his head. He grabbed June by his jacket and pulled him towards the car. "What are we going to do about the lug nuts?"

June let himself be pulled along, happy to go wherever James Kelly wanted him. Instead of getting into the car, he sprawled across the front of the Rambler, looking up at the stars. He tugged James Kelly down with him. "We'll put out an offering. If we've got anything to offer."

"What's that?"

"Don't worry about it." June scooted closer to him. James Kelly let him. He was always cuddlier and less skittish right after he'd fed. "I'd like to do something for you."

"I..." James Kelly bit his lip, swallowed, then sighed. He hugged June, bringing him close. "You did. And I don't know about anything else right now."

"Alright." June didn't think he was being distant or anything like that but imagined he was genuinely sated by what they'd done and perhaps a little overwhelmed. "Have you looked at the stars?"

"Hmm?"

"Look." June nodded up towards the stars. They were smaller and duller than they had been the first time he'd seen them, but brighter and more numerous than they were anywhere in New York City.

The vampire turned his eyes towards the sky and June could see all the stars reflected against the pale golden brown of his irises, a million specks of light. June couldn't help but imagine what he'd look like rendered in soft colors, an oil painting hung in a museum where, in a hundred years, people would come to wonder what such a beautiful man had been like.

James Kelly claimed he had been an awkward-looking child and June didn't know that Anastasia had ever appreciated for what he was, instead of who he could replace. From what June had heard, she'd given a lot of backhanded compliments, saying that his nose wasn't too curved, that he wasn't too dark, that his hair wasn't too rough, that it was good he could comb and style his hair, otherwise, he'd look like a wildman. She had liked to compare him to Swiss chocolate, which had always felt inaccurate and too much like she was bragging.

It made James Kelly prickly about how things were worded, now that he'd started to speak up for himself a little more, so June tried to keep his compliments clear-cut.

"An offering to what?" James Kelly murmured, still gazing towards the sky.

"To whoever took our lug nuts."

His mouth tugged down and he turned his eyes towards June. "What do you mean?"

June slid off the front of the Rambler and went inside it, rummaging through for whatever he could find that might pass as an offering. He found a mashed-up Twinkie under one seat; he had bought a box on a whim and had stopped half-way through one when he'd realized that the filling was vanilla, instead of banana like it had used to be.

James Kelly had eaten the rest of the box, except for this one, and had scowled mightily when June had teased him about not eating anything but sweets.

June unwrapped it and placed it on a bit of cardboard. He took it over to the oak tree and hoped the Fair Folk considered their display earlier amusing rather than offensive.

James Kelly continued to frown at him and when he came back to the car, asked, "What, you think a raccoon took them?"

"No!" June laughed. "Come on in the car. Aren't you cold?"

They waited in the car, talking and smoking, cracking the windows when the car filled up with too much smoke.

"So how many girls has your mom tried to set you up with?"

"Three."

June's eyebrows shot up. "Three! It's only been a couple months."

"Three in January. I haven't...you know, that's sort of when I stopped taking her calls," he confessed.

"Ah." June stubbed his cigarette out in the ashtray and immediately took out another. "Well." He took a few drags. "I haven't got a mother."

"You mentioned."

"Well, it's just that normally I've got a lot of experience with things. And I haven't got any with this."

"What...uh. What about your father?"

June glanced upwards, more of an eye roll, really. "Him? He's...He made me. He's my father, you know, in that sense but in the same way that He's your father. So I've got God but I never had a Harold."

"Maybe you aren't supposed to tell me, but...uh. You talk about Heaven like you miss it sometimes. So why...?"

"Why did we fall?" June guessed. Everyone asked that eventually. "There's a lot of answers for that. I can't speak for my king, I can't even start to fathom what's going on in that head of his. He was always more complicated than I am."

"Then what about just you?"

"Maybe you won't like my answer," June replied cagily. The car suddenly felt small. "Maybe it's not so easy to explain these things."

"Try."

"I..." June licked his lips and examined his unnaturally stubby nails, wishing for them to be claws again. There were answers, half-truths that made perfect sense. Lying felt wrong, though, in a lot of ways. "I love him."

James Kelly's head tilted the side ever so slightly, a dangerous angle, especially when combined with his narrowed eyes.

"I want to say it's not like that, but...it is and it isn't. And I don't like to talk about it. But, well, you ought to know anyway. He's my king, I am loyal to him. That's about the only thing that's never changed."

James Kelly went on not saying anything.

"It's this ache when you've wanted something you can't ever have, that you never could. There was never anything either of us could do about it. You get used to it but sometimes it aches a little more than usual. So that's why I fell. I loved him more than I loved God." June brought his cigarette to his lips but found that it had gone to ash while he'd been talking. "Go on, say something about it, why don't you?"

"There's nothing for me to say."

"Aren't you angry?"

"I don't know."

"You're always angry," June accused, knowing how childish he was being.

That clouded James Kelly's face and a foul thrill of delight moved through June, followed by a sense of nausea. He had never been good at fighting this way and he didn't want to start now.

"Like I said, though, we'll never be together and...you know, even if we could now, I think the time's passed for anything. It's...just how things are. And you haven't got to go worrying about playing second fiddle or anything. I love you and that about all there is to it. Do you believe me?"

"I think I do," James Kelly told him, sounding more than a little surprised with himself.

June smiled, but it felt forced and nervous. He lit a cigarette. The bite on his arm itched and sort of throbbed. He rubbed it through his jacket.

"How are you feeling?"

"I feel fine. You hardly took any," June assured.

James Kelly made eye contact for a half a second, then blushed and looked at his hands. Not a moment later, though, he was sneaking a glance up at June, his bottom lip caught between his teeth.

"You're begging to be kissed, looking at me like that."

"No, I..." He shrugged. "I don't know."

Unable to stop a smile from spreading across his face, June asked, "What?"

"It just, well. I never...I've never done anything like that."

"Didn't imagine you had."

James Kelly squirmed and June extended a hand, which the vampire took with both of his, knotting their fingers together. "I don't want to talk about it."

"Oh." June went cold all of a sudden and it didn't have anything to do with the breeze coming in through the cracked window. He took his hand back.

James Kelly grabbed at him, catching him by the wrist and holding on. "No, no, not, not like that. Not like I didn't like it or like it was...*wrong* but...I don't know. I just don't want to talk about it. Not until I've had time to think."

The cold feeling faded a little. "Oh."

"Cause I know..." He rubbed the back of his neck. "I *know* when I get mixed up, when I don't have time to think about what I want to say I, I say them wrong. I sound stupid—"

"You don't."

"So I get embarrassed and—"

"And you start shouting."

"Would you let me finish!" James Kelly snapped, then realized that he'd raised his voice. He sighed and rubbed his mouth, then curled up his fingers and pressed his fist against his lips. "I'm sorry. I am," he whispered.

June inched closer and placed his hand on James Kelly's knee. "Take as much time as you need." He put his hand atop the vampire's head and gave it an affectionate wobble. "Give all those thoughts a chance to get together. You're probably trying to use too many of those big words of yours."

James Kelly ducked his head away, a hint of a smile on his face.

June drew him in and kissed the side of his face. "When you know what you want to say, I'll be listening."

Looping his arms around June's neck, James Kelly let out a sigh. "I love you."

June grinned and teased, "It took you months to get that thought together!"

James Kelly said nothing else, not to defend himself or tease back, but he brought June in closer. June twisted in his arms so that he could still smoke.

Hours passed and June's stomach started to rumble. He smoked all his cigarettes and dozed on and off until James Kelly shook him awake and hissed, "June, did you hear that?"

"Mmm?"

"Something fell on the car."

"Mmm." June nestled into his arms, then sat up. "Oh!" He scampered out of the car and found that the lug nuts scattered around the car.

James Kelly followed him, watching as June rushed around picking them up. "What...?"

"Goddamn fairies!" June exclaimed, no longer worried about angering them and running the risk of never getting the lug nuts back.

"Fairies?" James Kelly leaned out the window, his face still drawn.

Something pulled his hair and he checked his urge to swat it away. Instead, he rushed to finish changing the tire. "Don't tell Marie I said that, either, it'd be the end of me."

As soon as the tire was secure, he had them back on the road, driving faster than was advisable, but he didn't want to linger anywhere that had prankster fairies for much longer.

Once he felt the risk of running into any more fairies, he slowed down, thinking that running into police would likely be just as bad.

MARCH 18, 1954.

Daybreak found June in just about his least favorite place in New York state, aside from one pizzeria in East Harlem, where he'd made the mistake of kind of coming on to Tony Grimaldi and gotten a fat lip and a pair of broken ribs for his trouble. Wei had been the only thing between him and a real beating that night. It had been something to see Wei, who normally kept out of other people's troubles, spitting mad, storming into the backroom with a chair leg in one hand and a fireball in the other. He'd cracked Tony across the head and singed all the hair off one of his buddies before hauling June's sorry ass out of the place.

June momentarily considered sharing the story with James Kelly but dismissed the idea in less than a second. It wouldn't do anything but confirm what the vampire already assumed would happen if he dared to so much as mention Truman Capote.

When he thought about it a little more, he didn't actually know if James Kelly had read anything by Capote. "Hey?"

"Hmm?"

"You ever read any of Truman Capote's stuff?"

"Annie read *The Grass Harp*. Or, well, she started it."

"But did you read it?"

"No, I figure I'll get around to it someday," the vampire answered with a shrug.

He'd torn through *Nineteen Eighty-Four* already and had been working on a *Doc Savage* novel that he'd found in the trunk. Wei read pulp novels like business men read *The Wall Street Journal.*

June cut the engine. He had slept well last night and hadn't had a lick of trouble getting out of bed, but now that he was here, he wanted to be elsewhere. Even the land had a sour feel to it and the trees themselves were gnarled, stunted things. For five years, June had tried his best to help them grow and for five years, the results had been a weak crop.

A soft, doughy woman walked out to greet him; she had a sallow face that might have been pleasant once, but now was marked with fatigue and ill-health. A pudgy little boy toddled along beside her, red-cheeked and clumsy. "Mr. Lyons is out. He'll be back in about an hour, I figure."

June nodded. He still hadn't worked out if this woman was a wife or a servant or what, but the child didn't bear much of a resemblance to the hard, lean man that was Joshua Lyons. Of course, this was the most he'd ever heard her say in half a decade.

"Should I, uh...should I go ahead and get started?" he asked.

She patted the boy on his head and looked out towards the trees. "Mr. Lyons says to tell you if you can't figure it out this time not to bother coming back next year."

June raised his eyebrows. Lyons had always insisted that the land could be wrangled into submission. "What made him change his mind?"

"He's got the idea into his head that the land's cursed. Fixing to declare bankruptcy if you can't get things growing."

"Wouldn't the Hubbards buy it back?"

She let out a weak cackle. "He'd sooner die." She peered into the car. "He won't be too happy to see that."

It took June a lot of staring and puzzling to figure out that she must have meant James Kelly. "He'll have to cope as best he can."

She shrugged and head back towards the house. Under her breath, June thought he heard her say, "Your funeral."

June couldn't blame Lyons for thinking the land was cursed and June wouldn't have been surprised if it had been. Lyons' wife had been a Hubbard and the land had been hers by inheritance. It had been good land no more than ten years ago and had only really started to go to shit after she'd died.

The Hubbards had offered to buy back the orchard but Lyons had accused them of trying to cheat him. Or, as June had heard it, of trying to Jew him.

Maybe it would be better if James Kelly didn't have to meet him.

June went over to the window and tapped on it.

James Kelly rolled it down. "What?"

"Uh. Well. Keys are in the car if you wanted to go for a drive."

The vampire squinted at him. "Why?"

"Cause the fellow who owns it is...uh...He's not too keen, well, he's one of those sorts that's, um..."

"In the Klan?" James Kelly guessed. "I've sort of been waiting for one to pop up out here in the middle of nowhere."

"I don't know if he's paying dues but they wouldn't turn him down if he applied."

"Imagine if the Klan collected dues," the vampire mused. "What do you think they'd spend them on? Renting out halls for Christmas parties or buying rope wholesale?" He rolled the window back up and locked the door, giving June a smile before he settled back into the seat with his arms crossed and his eyes closed.

Dawn had barely broken and the vampire had been drowsy the whole way over. He peeked open one eye after a bit, then waved June away.

Instinct pushed June to argue, but reason doubted that Lyons would do anything drastic.

And, June thought as he took his suitcase from the trunk, James Kelly was a vampire and as such he definitely could hold his own in a fight, especially against a human.

The woman hadn't invited him inside, so he spread out his kit on some stiff, prickly grass near the house to sort through everything and find what he needed. The containers were remarkably less organized than they had been on the way out of the city. He chose to blame the cow that had knocked the suitcase over and not his own negligence.

The little boy crept out the front door and watched June from the front steps, his chubby face drawn and quiet. Eventually, June couldn't resist and looked his way, giving a little wave and a smile.

The boy widened his eyes and drew his hands close to his chest, his little mouth puckered in concern.

"What's wrong?" June asked.

"You're gonna eat me?"

"No."

"Mommy says monsters eat babies."

"I don't."

The child didn't look convinced.

"I promise."

"What do you eat?"

"Lots of things. What do you eat?"

"I don't know. Maybe...eggs sometimes."

"Oh."

The child went quiet, studying his little hands as though they might be able to tell him what to do. "Mommy says not to talk to you."

"Alright."

"She says there's devils in the trees."

June didn't think she was wrong. There was something fundamentally *not right* about this place. He wondered what Lyons got up to out here, or what the Hubbards had been doing differently when it had been their land.

He wondered but didn't want to go poking around to find out.

To the child, he said, "There's only one Devil and he doesn't hang around in trees."

Pointing to June's suitcase, the boy asked, "What's those?"

June lifted up a few of the jars so the boy could see them more clearly and after one more question, he launched into an eager explanation of what he'd brought with him. Almost no one asked how he did what he did, they just handed over his payment and send him away, worried about spending too much time with a demon.

He'd also never been able to deny a child an answer to whatever question they asked. The world was a vast place, full of infinite wonders, though it had taken June a while to sort out what things children weren't supposed to be told.

"Joshua!" the woman shrieked, barreling out of the house, frantically searching for the boy.

Her eyes landed on him crouched beside June's suitcase, holding a jar of glittering green sand. June was seated next to him and had been explaining that it had taken a four-hour ritual on a midsummer afternoon to get it to glitter like that.

She clattered down the stairs and grabbed the little boy by the arm, squeezing so hard his fat squished up between her fingers. "How dare you!" she snarled at June, spit flying from her mouth.

He recoiled, leaning back and bracing himself against the ground.

She dragged the child up into her arms. "He's a *baby*."

The jar slipped from his grasp and shattered on the ground. His chubby face scrunched up but any cries he might have given were muffled by his mother's breast as she clutched him close.

"A *baby*."

June didn't know what to say. He didn't know what she thought he had been doing. "I, uh..."

"Disgusting," she accused.

"I wasn't...I..." He'd spent about half an hour with the boy, showing him all the prettier things he kept in jars and vials and he realized that she must have spent that half-hour scouring the house for her son. It explained the prickles of anxiety that had been winding around the area, ones that he'd brushed aside as part of the whole area's queasy feel.

He pushed himself to her feet and approached, arms spread to show how harmless he was.

"You faggots, you're all the same," she hissed.

So that was it.

"As bad as he is!" This time her voice came out strident, high and loud enough to set birds awing.

He wondered who she meant but knew better than to ask. Normally mothers trusted him, but there was a rabid protectiveness about this woman. Someone'd hurt her baby and she'd never trust another with him again.

"Peace, missus," he attempted. "Faggot I might be, but he's a babe and I'd rather lose a hand than do him harm." He hoped he sounded genuine, tried to put honesty and goodwill into his voice.

A car door open and June chanced a look towards the Rambler. James Kelly had exited the car but hadn't approached them.

"You'll do what he pays you for and get out," the woman warned.

June nodded and made the foolish mistake of taking a step towards her. He wasn't used to distrust, not on this level, and it was hard for him to check his instinct to provide comfort by laying on hands. He had meant to do nothing more than gesture towards the house, tell her to go inside and lock the door, but a heavy blow to the jaw knocked him back.

"Stay. Away."

He threw up his hands, flinching, but she didn't hit him again.

The little boy had started to really cry, loud enough to be heard no matter how he was smothered against his mother's chest. James Kelly had walked away from the Rambler, crossing the crunchy yellow grass to put himself between June and the woman.

He slid his body between the two of them, his face twisted into a nasty snarl and his shoulders squared. June grabbed him by the shoulder, pulled him back before the vampire could growl anything at her.

"No, no, leave her," June insisted. "Don't."

A strangled cry of frustration escaped James Kelly as he spared half a glance for June, still keeping an eye on the woman. If June hadn't been so worried, he would have been squarely between amused and touched.

"Go inside, missus, lock the door," June told her. "I haven't come here to do you harm, I swear it."

She didn't get the chance to accept or deny the truth in his words. A truck came up the drive, parking beside the Rambler.

Lyons stalked towards them and June expected accusations to come flying, thought that the woman would spit that he had done all kinds of foul things to the child, but instead, the woman withdrew from them, heading towards the house, clutching the crying child to her breast.

"What's been going on?" Lyons demanded of her.

"Nothing."

He glared between the three of them, his eyes settling

dangerously on James Kelly. "You letting niggers on my land?"

She protested, "I didn't—"

He turned from her. "Less you're *owned,* boy, you got no right on my land," Lyons warned. "So you'd best go."

His eyes, pale and hard, slid over James Kelly in a bizarre way, full of disgust and hate and something else.

The woman completed her retreat to the house, shushing the little boy. June would have sworn he heard the door lock.

James Kelly glanced at June and June didn't know what to do.

"You want to be owned?" Lyons asked.

It was a disquieting question and the man's voice held an unsettling mix of threat and anticipation, like he wanted James Kelly to give him lip, give him permission to see him as a threat. It let June identify that other thing lurking behind his eyes. It wasn't lust, not exactly, but it was kin, it was the need to defile something, to hate it and use it.

"I'll show you what you're good for, boy."

It happened before June could really process. James Kelly spat a thick glob right onto the man's face and Lyons grabbed him by the throat, hard enough that the vampire lost his footing and slid back a few inches.

"You're gonna wish—"

"Let him go," June warned. Frightened mothers he could forgive but not this. When Lyons didn't move fast enough, he gave the man a shove away from James Kelly, who mustn't have needed protecting but might have wanted it.

Lyons roared, "You're not coming on to *my—*"

June raised his hand towards the sky and pulled down a bit of punishment, something he had never tried before. He'd always suspected that he had this power, but calling down a pestilence wasn't exactly his style and he didn't exactly relish the idea of being the kind of demon that went around cursing people.

As he spoke, he didn't feel like himself, he felt slippery and far away. "You'll fix your ways, Joshua Lyons, or you'll die before the year is out. Your trees with die with you. You'll rot outside in. The skin, the muscles, the bone. You'll make amends and mean them or you'll rot to death. Your punishment is sealed."

He'd been made to help but this didn't feel like helping. It felt wrong, but he had done it anyway.

Lyons staggered when June pronounced it, like the words had actual weight, and that God-awful feeling stopped sliding over June's skin. He didn't know how long that would last or how many guns he would retrieve from his house when he came to his senses, so he hastened to pack up his suitcase and pushed James Kelly towards the Rambler.

James Kelly hesitated, his eyes fixed on Lyons, and June put his hand on the small of his back and shoved, hard enough to break the trance but not enough to get him moving.

"You can't kill him," June reminded, taking him by the hand.

James Kelly wrinkled his nose. "I don't want to kill him!"

"Then let's *go*." He pulled at him again and James Kelly came with him all the way to the car.

"June," James Kelly pronounced severely as the backed down the drive.

"I can drive, I'm alright."

"June, what did you *do* to him?"

"I..."

"I've never seen you like that before. What was that!"

"He...he needed to be punished."

Wary, almost frightened, James Kelly said, "I thought you weren't that sort of demon."

"I'm not."

"Well, then....!"

"I'm not but I can be," June amended. "When my king made me Watcher, he made it...he gave me the power to do more than just watch."

"Shit."

"I know."

James Kelly cleared his throat. "If you're not that kind of demon, what's got you...uh, well, handing out punishments like that?"

"I don't know."

"Sounded awful like you put a curse on him if you ask me."

"I did."

"Why?"

June didn't know, not exactly; he knew that Lyons was a foul man and that he'd intended to harm James Kelly. More than just harm him, really, Lyons had wanted to do awful things to him. When he'd put his hands on the vampire, June had gotten the image of James Kelly chained and ruined, subject to all kinds of abuses and physically able to bear all of the, beyond what any mortal man could.

He didn't know if it had been his imagination or a glimpse into Lyons' intentions, a bit of insight provided by whatever authority his king had granted him.

"He has to change. And he shouldn't have grabbed you."

A minute passed, the world around them calm and beautiful, the feeling in the car unsettled.

"How's your face?" James Kelly asked.

"Fine."

"What'd that woman go and hit you for?"

"Oh, she thought I was trying something with the kid."

James Kelly scowled and grumbled something to himself about goddamn McCarthy and goddamn idiots. He smacked the dashboard once then settled back into his seat, arms crossed.

June couldn't help reliving what had happened in his head, his thoughts always coming back to settle on how James Kelly had rushed to defend him. It filled him up with all sorts of warm feelings, some of it nothing more than affection, but a large part of it was attraction. He'd looked so *good* rushing over like that.

It made him fidgety and James Kelly must have noticed because he kept throwing glances toward June.

He brought them to the motel where they'd planned to stay the night anyway; it was a small, out of the way place that he'd known for years. A place that was just about as queer-friendly as it got these days, considering that it was owned by a couple of men who'd been claiming to be cousins for years now.

One of the owners raised his eyebrows at June when he came into the office, his gaze flicking to James Kelly for a second. "Mr. Thompson, is it that time of year already?"

"Feels like it hasn't been more than six months," he said. "How've you been, Horace?"

"Wonderful."

"And Richard?"

"Miserable, like he always is. One room?" Horace inquired, pulling out the guestbook.

June couldn't help the stupid smile that crawled across his face and he nodded.

James Kelly gave the two of them a sideways look and put a little more distance between himself and June.

"But two beds, of course," Horace said, his voice full of mock condemnation.

June snorted, scribbled their names in the book, and took the keys that Horace offered him.

During the whole walk to their room, June felt jumpy, almost nervous, in a way he hadn't in a long time.

As soon as the door closed June dropped his suitcases, not caring about the unpleasant rattle one of them gave off; if something was broken, he'd clean it up later.

He caught James Kelly's face in his hands and kissed him, getting as close as he could. The other man melted against him after a brief moment of shock. He wound his hands into June's shirt, pulling him even more so that June had to rock forward on his toes or risk toppling forward.

When they separated, breathing hard, June touched his forehead to James Kelly's.

"What's gotten into you?" the vampire panted, not angry but pleased, maybe a little amused.

"You're beautiful."

He rolled his eyes.

June kissed him again. "You are, God, I've never seen anyone so lovely."

"In a thousand years?"

"In two thousand, at least! I swear you keep getting better-looking, you human things. All your teeth and not a touch of pox."

James Kelly snorted and put a hand on June's chest, giving him a push back and turning away. He shrugged off his jacket and lay it on the bed, keeping his back to June.

June didn't think he'd respond too well to having someone come up behind him, so he came around to his front again. "Come on, let me show you how much I like you."

He glanced over.

June looked back, making eye contact and hoping that he looked earnest and love-struck. He couldn't quite read the look on James Kelly's face. "Or tell me off if I'm bothering you."

"I..."

"Tell me what to do," June pleaded.

James Kelly sucked in a breath and June thought he'd been too forward, made him nervous. James Kelly cleared his throat and whispered, "I'd like it if..." He cleared his throat.

"Go on, honey," June urged, trying to sound as gentle as he could. He had plenty of patience, especially when it came to James Kelly. *Don't over think it*, he wanted to say, but thought it would be better if he didn't blabber too much.

"Maybe you could go down on me."

June nodded, his heart leaping up into his throat in the best way possible. He grabbed him by the wrist and pulled him into the bed; his hands shook, excited and nervous. He'd never had permission to do anything like this for James Kelly. He slid on top of the vampire and started undoing his tie, unbuttoning the shirt, intending to get him out of as much clothing as possible.

James Kelly put his hands on June's chest and June hesitated, waiting for the push back, expecting a change of heart, but James Kelly pushed June's jacket off his shoulders and tugged his shirt over his head, giggling when it snagged on his horns. Before June even had time to be embarrassed, though, James Kelly soothed him with a kiss.

As they stripped away each other's clothes, June realized that, yes, they'd been naked together before, but not like this. All their snippets of kissing and petting had been mostly clothed and even their showers together had been overwhelmingly tame; he'd hadn't had so much of James Kelly's skin against his when they were both warmed from kissing. June thought about suggesting more, slavishly offering to do whatever James Kelly wanted, but stopped himself. The vampire was new to this, in some sense, and had named his request. It would be stupid, not to mention morally dicey, to try anything else.

He did take the opportunity to kiss him all over, his throat and stomach, his ribs and thighs, letting his tongue sneak out every so often to trace over his skin.

When he'd gotten his fill of kissing, he looked up to James Kelly, who'd been sighing delightfully the whole time, little sounds of pleasure getting caught in his throat. "Should I...?"

He nodded and June grinned, glad for the chance and gladder still when he lowered his head and was able to elicit plaintive little moans and cries from the other man. A thousand stupid thoughts flitted through his head, memories of past lovers, of things they didn't know about each other, of whether or not James Kelly would dance with him at the festival.

The taste when he spilled surprised him; June had done this with a few vampires before, the product of too much drinking and the need to connect with anyone, and the taste of their seed had always been flat, dead, and it caught him unaware to discover that James Kelly didn't taste like that.

Maybe because he hadn't been dead for very long or because he wasn't as dead as the others, maybe just because he'd had his fill of blood recently. Whatever the reason, he tasted alive.

He slid back up beside him, ready to nestle close and maybe take a nap, but James Kelly seemed to have other ideas. He hooked a leg around June, kissed him hard, and slipped his hands between June's legs, coaxing him towards his own climax. He barely noticed when James Kelly's teeth scraped against his shoulder.

"Do you mind?"

June didn't know what he was supposed to be minding, so he said, "No."

He realized what he'd consented to when he felt a small bite, not any deeper than a cat scratch and devotedly attended to by the vampire's mouth. This he could easily get used to.

James Kelly crooned that he loved him, his lips moving against June's skin, his tongue running over the bite to lap up the small drops of blood that oozed out. He caught June's mouth in another kiss, which was enough to bring him over the edge.

They stayed close together, their skin cooling, until James Kelly wiggled his way under the covers, murmuring, "It's chilly in here, hasn't this place got heat?"

June kissed his cheek. "I'll be right back," he promised and headed to the bathroom, thinking of what they could do with the rest of their day. It would have taken hours to do the Lyons orchard and now the rest of the morning and afternoon stretched in front of them.

He washed his hands and wiped clean the bite on his shoulder, then jumped out of his skin when he reached for the door and brushed black silk instead.

He dropped to his knees, his heart still hammering in his chest. "My king." He touched his forehead to the floor.

Before him loomed the Devil, lanky and pale, his fingers knotted in his hair. "Rise," the Devil told him.

He obeyed.

Lucifer's eyes slid over him; he probed at the bite with one skinny finger. "Hm."

"Why...?"

Lucifer nodded towards the bedroom. "He's nodded off. Absolutely precious, I have to say. And besides, I need to talk with you."

June sighed. "In the bathroom."

"You should thank me for my consideration, I had half a mind to interrupt you."

Heat crept over his face. "What do you require of me?"

"An explanation." The Devil buried his hands in his pockets and leaned against the bathroom door.

June rubbed the back of his neck. "About...?"

"You know perfectly well what about."

"I didn't...I didn't really think about it, I just did it. He was a foul man anyway, deserved to be cursed or, or whatever it was you gave me the power to do."

"His soul was already marked, you know."

June's eyes widened.

"He sold it years ago to someone else. And now you've gone and put *my* mark on him."

"I'm sorry, I didn't, I had no idea."

"Tell me why you did it. All of it, the whole story."

June shifted on one foot, then related what had happened. The Devil listened, his face sober and his eyes trained on June's.

Finally, when the telling was done, Lucifer sighed and rubbed his eyes. "Fine."

"Fine?"

"Fine, I think I can make a case out of it. Shouldn't be enough to start a war over—"

"A war!" June squeaked.

"Shouldn't," Lucifer repeated. "You know it's your responsibility now. In a year, to go back and clean up whatever becomes of him and whatever he does because of your...let's call it a warning."

June had not known that. The only word that came to mind was, "Oh."

"I'll have the paperwork sent over when it's time." He poked again at the bite on June's shoulder. "Good for you. Relationships look good on you."

The corner of June's mouth tipped up.

"Anyway, I've got to go."

June nodded.

"Well, give me a hug," he demanded.

June wrapped his arms around the Devil, squeezing hard. Lucifer kissed the top of his head, then stepped back.

As soon as he had come, Lucifer was gone, leaving June melancholy but glad to have seen him. He sidled under the covers with James Kelly and wrapped an arm around him, careful not to wake him. Less guarded in sleep than he ever was awake, the vampire twisted around and burrowed into his arms, leaving June to realize just how bad he had it for James Kelly.

Bad enough that all the ache of seeing the Devil subsided as soon as the vampire mumbled, "Love you," into his chest.

Well. Almost all of it, anyway.

March 19, 1954.

The full moon loomed above them; they were out so deep in the forest that the Milky Way cut a swath across the sky, illuminating the path through the trees. Anyone who wandered off the narrow dirt path on a night like this ran the risk of falling right through reality, so June kept a guiding hand on James Kelly's shoulder.

They reached a clearing the size of a baseball field and June bumped into the vampire, who had stopped walking. Past him, June could see that the bonfire that climbed towards the sky and saw at least a dozen people with flutes and drums, their music winding into the forest. People were already dancing, the beat of the music quick but not frenzied.

"You can go on," June urged.

"I don't know."

"Do you want me to walk you back to the car?"

They'd parked at the foot of the mountain with everyone else who'd driven and hiked about an hour up to reach the clearing. The whole time James Kelly had been peppering him with questions and June got the sense that the vampire had been avoiding the topic for days.

"No."

June hugged him from behind and kissed his cheek. "I absolutely promise you that no one here will give you trouble for being queer or colored or Jewish *or* a vampire."

James Kelly stepped out of his grasp. "You never know, though."

June tried to be sympathetic. It was a large crowd, probably the most creatures that James Kelly had ever encountered all in one place. Even Peggy's New Year's Eve party hadn't had so many. "We'll hold hands," he offered.

James Kelly shook his head and stepped into the clearing, his hands in his pockets and his shoulders hunched.

June walked beside him, struggling to match his slow place. Everything about this place called to him. He wanted to dance around the fire and drink too much, he wanted to throw his power out into the land to make things fertile and rich and good. He also sort of wanted to take his clothes off.

Instead, he found drinks for the two of them and stood beside James Kelly, watching the others.

"Fairies," June said, nodding towards a few revelers in various shades of blue, green, and purple. His gaze flicked through the crowd again and he spied a woman with hair the color of autumn leaves and skin like birch bark. She had her own dais of pine boughs and seemed to have brought a lot of courtiers with her. He elbowed James Kelly. "Maeve."

"Hmm?"

"She's queen of one of the kingdoms in the Otherworld."

"Oh." The vampire didn't seem particularly interested.

"I've known her for years. She lived in my borough for a little while, before she got the throne. Central Park."

"Central Park has fairies?"

"Lousy with them!" June declared. "How do you think Marie's parents met?"

The contorted look on his face told June that James Kelly had never considered how Marie's parents had met.

"Bound to be a fun night with fairies here. You've got to step careful around them, mind your manners, you know. And, well, hopefully, there aren't any here that hold grudges." It was a useless hope; fairies always held grudges.

"Grudges?"

"Uh, well, you know, fairies and demons didn't get off on the right foot after the Fall. Younger ones might not hold a grudge. I can't say for sure. They're...mercurial."

James Kelly nodded.

June tugged on his elbow. "Come on, let's say hi. I think you'll like her."

The vampire acquiesced, following him and even imitating June's bow.

"Something told me you'd be here," Maeve said, smiling warmly at June as he climbed the dais.

She spread her arms and he gave her a quick embrace, kissing her cheek. He made introductions, though he skirted around calling James Kelly his boyfriend or companion, knowing that it might set him even more on edge.

With a shrug and a grin, he told her, "You know me, I always turn up."

"I think I owe you an apology."

"I can't think of any offense," he assured.

"No? Something about that horrible iron trap you ride around in, I think."

"Oh!" He laughed. "The lug nuts. No, all returned, just a little bit of a delay. Right?" He glanced towards the vampire, who only nodded.

"You shouldn't run into any more mischief. I've had words with my court."

"Your Majesty, I appreciate it."

She assured, "They were children, really, they haven't grown into their manners yet."

He grinned. Young fairies were always troublemakers, though they hardly ever meant to sow chaos or do any harm. "Well, you know how children are."

She put her hand on his arm.

After a few drinks, June was sure that James Kelly would lighten up. He thought he might even be able to get him to dance before the sun was up.

Except James Kelly barely sipped at his drink. He stood stiffly off to the side while June chatted with the fairy queen. He sat once Maeve offered him a seat, the same drink clasped between his hands. The cup rested on his knee.

June didn't think he should be pushing him to drink, but couldn't help it. He prodded and nudged James Kelly through at least two drinks, knowing that the vampire was growing irritated with him.

He spied a mop of peach pink curls whirling through the crowd around the bonfire. The sight made his stomach twist and threaten to turn out the four drinks he'd swallowed. The owner of the curls locked eyes with him mid-twirl and stopped dead, then pushed through the crowd, his dandelion yellow cheeks flushed and his eyes sparkling.

"June!" he cried, rushing over. "Junie, I kept hoping I'd see you here! How *are* you?"

June knew that Kaveon was asking with real concern, especially since last time they'd seen each other, June had been recently stabbed. The time before that, Kaveon had been breaking up with him. "I'm fine."

"You look great, really! What are you doing standing over here?"

June rubbed his nose and tried not to cast a blameful look towards James Kelly. All of him ached to be among the other dancers. "Just watching, I guess."

Kaveon threw back his head and laughed. He took June by the hand and gave him a pull towards the fire. "Come on, dance with me."

"I..." Every instinct said to go with him, hundreds of years of friendship and a long time as lovers. He knew exactly how Kaveon would twist his slender body like a stalk in the wind, how he would jump and laugh, what his mouth would taste like. June had influence over fertility and Kaveon over sex; they'd been a pair even in Heaven before either of them had gotten bodies. "I'm here with someone."

"Bring him, too!"

"Kavi."

"I'll be *very, very* good, Junie, I promise," he vowed. He gestured towards the crowd. "Look, no one's even fucking, I'm being incredibly restrained."

"How's Liz?" June asked, reminding him of the wife he had, of the family he'd started and for which he'd left June behind. Kaveon and his wife had been monogamous for centuries.

Kaveon's face fell. He rubbed the back of his neck. "You don't want to get into that."

"I sort of do," June admitted.

"Then I need a drink, I'll be right back." Kaveon danced off and June thought that would be the last he'd see of him.

"Isn't that your ex?" came a small, sour voice from his side.

June nodded. "He'll forget all about me," he assured.

James Kelly huffed.

"What?"

"I didn't say anything," James Kelly sniffed.

"No, but...well, you're looking at me like that."

"I'm not looking at you like anything."

June chewed on his thumbnail, trying to think of something to say. "Do you want to dance with me?"

His back rigid and his voice stiff, the vampire answered, "No."

June nodded.

Kaveon returned with two drinks. He handed one to June and as he drank deeply from his own, his eyes lit on James Kelly. "Hi."

James Kelly drew in on himself. "Hello."

"Friend of June's?"

"Yes."

Kaveon beamed at him. "Wonderful. Always nice to meet someone new."

"We've met," James Kelly reminded.

"I'm sure it was wonderful to meet you then, too."

"Don't," June scolded. "Leave him alone."

"I'm just talking," Kavi insisted.

June put a hand on the other demon's arm. "Kavi, come on, you were telling me about Liz."

"Oh. Right." Kaveon took another drink and walked away, tugging on June's sleeve.

June asked James Kelly, "Want to come?"

"No."

"I'll be right there."

"Fine."

"It's only talking," he said, knowing how much he sounded like Kaveon in that moment. "I promise."

"Fine."

June sighed and went. Maybe some space would do the vampire some good. Maybe he and Maeve would get to talking. She was always good for all kinds of gossip and stories.

Kaveon had retreated to the edge of the clearing, no more than ten feet from the dais. He settled against a tree, one leg sprawled out in front of him, another tucked up near his chest. He had his drink resting on his thigh.

June sat beside him, legs crossed Indian-style. "How's Liz?"

Kaveon sighed. "You really don't want to hear about Liz."

"Has something bad happened to her?"

"No."

"Then I want to hear about it," June insisted, feeling entitled to know what had become of the woman who'd been more important than him.

"You know Mylas?"

"Sure, but he's dead. Been dead years."

"He's got this son. Well. Adopted son, you know Mylas never did it with girls. Harrison."

June waited, taking a sip of his drink, trying not to smile.

"He and Liz...you know, I really played my cards wrong with this! Anyway, Liz and Harry, they've been playing bridge."

"Christ, not bridge!" June pretended to be outraged.

"Shut up, Junie. They've been playing every weekend for months."

"So she's got friends. What's wrong with that?"

"They're fucking," Kaveon said.

"Ah."

"And she hasn't told me about it. She's been, uh, she's been sleeping in the guest room some nights, too."

"Have you talked to her about it?" June asked.

"I tried."

"Didn't go well?"

"Not even a little." Kaveon drained his cup and tossed it aside. He let his head loll against the tree and looked up. "She thinks I've been lying to her, too. About sleeping with other people. I told her I haven't been."

"Have you been?"

"No! I'm *not* a liar," the other demon insisted. "So she thinks I've been screwing around behind her back. Asked me to move out last week."

"Why does she think you've been going behind her back?"

"I don't know! If I knew I would fix it."

June nodded.

"And! And it's not like I, well, you know, it's not like it's been *easy*. In my line of work, there's a lot of opportunities and some of them are really good-looking opportunities. Turned them down every time for *three centuries*."

June didn't know what to tell him. "Things fall apart sometimes."

Kaveon rubbed his eyes. "I told her I didn't care that she was sleeping with someone else and I don't think that's what she wanted to hear. I think she wanted me to be jealous."

"Likely."

"Humanity. You think you've got a grasp on their stupid little minds and then..." Kaveon made a frustrated, sweeping gesture with his hands. "Eddy thinks I've been neglecting her."

June shrugged. "I don't know what to tell you. You can stay away or try to make amends, it's up to you."

A few fat tears slid down the other man's face.

Without thinking, June reached over and brushed them away. "Come on, Kavi, don't be mawkish. You know how these things go. People fight, they make up. Do you love her still?"

"I don't know."

"Figure that out first. Everything goes from there."

Kaveon nodded. He cleared his throat. "Come on, there's a revel going on and here we are sitting in the dark! Dance with me."

June looked towards the dais. He could see James Kelly angled towards Maeve. "I came with someone."

"It will only be dancing. I swear it."

Kaveon looked so forlorn and no matter that they'd been lovers once, June had always been fond of him, cared about him for years. "Yes, alright, let me talk to him first."

A watery smile spread across Kaveon's face. June believed his promise that it would only be dancing and besides, the other demon didn't have the power to make anyone do something they didn't want to do in the first place.

June climbed back up on to the dais and crouched next to James Kelly. He kept his voice calm and low as he told him, "I'm going to go dance."

The vampire stared at him.

"I know we've agreed not to be with anyone else, so I swear that's all it is. It's only dancing."

"Fine."

"If you change your mind, come find me cause I'd love to be dancing with you."

James Kelly glared as though June had asked him to do something impossible, something that June should have known was impossible, like it would have been a lesser offense if he'd asked a man with no legs to dance.

"I won't have anything else to drink. I love you to death, James Kelly, but I can't sit here all night and watch this whole festival go on without me."

"I. Already. Said. Fine."

June nodded. He'd expected as much. He stood, stripped off his jacket, as well as his boots and socks, and went to Kaveon.

The other demon grabbed on to him, his grin back on his face, and they ran together towards the bonfire.

Dipping into the crowd of dancers was like sliding into a warm river, one full of beautiful things. It felt like Heaven and kissing and laughter, the kind where you couldn't stop and didn't want to.

Kaveon held on to him the entire time, absolutely glowing in the firelight. It brought June back to the days of temples and bacchanals and sacred prostitution.

His mouth grew dry and his limbs heavy, but he couldn't stop, didn't ever want to stop dancing like this. He felt like he could open himself up to the world and let it swallow him, soak into the soil and the sky so that he could become the rain and the sun.

The music took on a headier beat, pounding, almost throbbing, and Kaveon put his hands on June's hips, drawing him in closer. The people around them were grinding together, heaving, moaning, and June realized that they'd been letting too much of themselves leak out into the air. For miles around, animals would be rutting out of season and there would be premature blossoms on trees when the sun rose tomorrow, making branches droop with fruit sooner here than anywhere else in the state. Fruit that would be heartier, sweeter; June wanted to be around to taste that.

A kiss grazed across June's cheek. "Thinking about putting down roots?"

"Aren't I always?"

Kaveon had himself wrapped around June, hanging all over him like they were about to join the people writhing on the ground. Even the music had grown fainter now; June glanced over to see all of the musicians save for one flutist pressed together.

Kaveon giggled.

They stopped dancing but Kaveon didn't stop grinning. He raised his arms and the cries of those around him swelled, reaching towards ecstatic. June felt that need winding around him, deep in his belly and between his legs. He couldn't look away from Kaveon, his face beatific and wild in the firelight.

Kaveon pulled down his arms with a flourish and they all screamed, climaxing together, probably harder than any of them had in their entire lives.

The demon's grin faltered and he tottered to one side, his eyes fluttering closed. June caught him and glanced around, looking at just how many people he'd poured himself into. The other demon's skin was damp and suddenly all the smells around him came flooding in, mud and sweat and other fluids.

Not a woman here would be going home without a baby in her belly, even the ones who'd thought they'd never quicken.

Kaveon leaned against him. "I could use a drink."

The remaining flutist struck up a sleepy tune.

"How about some water?" June offered.

Kaveon nodded. "Do you remember when you used to carry me home?"

"I remember all of it."

"I remember how stupid I was!"

"Nothing we can do about it now," June said and as much as he wanted to hear Kaveon say he'd been wrong, that he should have stayed with June, he wanted this conversation to end.

His eyes flicked to the dais.

Most of the fairies were among the revelers, picking up their discarded clothes and throwing them up into the branches.

James Kelly sat beside Maeve, stone-faced, with June's jacket folded on his lap.

June approached but the vampire stood and walked away like he would strike out into the woods on his own. June released Kaveon and hurried after him, catching his arm before he could make it far.

"What's wrong?" June asked.

"Let go of me."

June let go of him but almost didn't. "I only danced."

"Is that what dancing looks like to you?"

"I would have rather been dancing with you," June reminded.

James Kelly's face twisted and June tensed, waiting for him to start shouting. "You're a piece of shit, you know that? Dragging me out here to the middle of fucking nowhere so you could make me watch you rub all over someone else."

"I didn't *make you* do anything! I didn't make you sit up there all night with a stick up your ass!" June's ears were ringing and he almost didn't realize he was shouting, too. "Am I supposed to spend the rest of my life being miserable just because you are!"

James Kelly said nothing, drawing in on himself. All the bluster had gone out of him, but June couldn't stop.

"All I ever do is try to help you, you know! I just want you to be happy and I get my head bit off for it, for everything I do. If you want to be alone and miserable, then you go ahead."

He waited for James Kelly to shout back, but he didn't. He just stared, looking like a lost kid again.

"So fucking go, if that's what you want. Go back to Brooklyn and marry whatever stupid fucking girl your mother can dredge out of the Hudson!"

James Kelly did go but not before he told June, "I never should have let you talk me into this, any of this faggot bullshit."

June kicked over a pile of shoes.

"Ouch," came Kaveon's voice.

June scowled at him. Kaveon had made his way onto the

abandoned dais and lounged on his side, watching June and James Kelly fight like it was a fascinating drama.

"So..."

"Shut up, Kavi."

The other demon grinned. "Well, alright, but will you at least come sit with me?"

June stalked over but Kaveon wasn't put off by his stormy mood. He wrapped his arms around June and pulled him down on to the dais.

"He'll be over it in the morning," Kaveon promised, his lips pressed to June's shoulder. "He was watching you the whole time you were dancing, you know."

June shrugged out of Kaveon's grip. He hadn't known. He had hardly spared a thought for the vampire while he'd danced. He sighed and rubbed his face. "Where's Maeve got to?"

Kaveon shrugged. "I don't know. Who ever does with fairies?" He put his arms around June again. "I'm not trying to have sex with you, you know, so you can relax."

June believed him; if Kaveon had been trying to have sex with him he would have been upfront about it. He leaned into his arms and dozed off.

He woke up hours later, still nestled with the other demon, stiff from the cold of the night. They had burrowed underneath someone else's jacket. He stood and stretched.

"Mmmm," Kaveon whined.

"I've got to piss, I'll be right back."

"Mmm."

June snagged his own jacket from the dais, finding it right where James Kelly had been sitting the whole time.

It wasn't James Kelly's fault, really, and June shouldn't have shouted at him like that. He contemplated all the other things he could have done, groggily realizing that he'd had more to drink than he should have. He propped himself up against a tree to have a leak, sloppily peed all over his feet, and sighed.

Outside the clearing, the fairies would surely be making trouble, but Maeve liked him, and he knew enough about fairies to generally avoid problems with them.

He could hear a stream bubbling nearby and made his way

over, dunking in his feet, which had been caked with mud and could have stood to be washed, even before he'd made a mess of himself.

At least, he reasoned, he hadn't thrown up. Or been thrown up on.

The ice of the water brought him back to his senses and he started to worry about where, exactly, James Kelly had gone. Distraught, alone, and in the middle of nowhere were not fantastic ways to find oneself, especially not if one had been drinking.

He heard a voice, sweet and low, coming from downstream and he followed it, recognizing it as Maeve. She would know where the vampire was and maybe she'd even be able to undo whatever trouble the vampire had stumbled upon.

Except that it seemed the trouble James Kelly had found was her. Both of them stood in the stream, lit up in the moonlight.

The vampire tottered unevenly and had the queen's fingers in his mouth.

June frowned and sloshed closer to them, not exactly sure he knew what was happening or why. He didn't think that James Kelly was the sort to sneak off into the woods and suck the fingers of anyone, let alone a fairy queen.

She withdrew her fingers and James Kelly fell to one knee, his head bowed.

"Looking for this?" Maeve asked, cupping James Kelly's face in her hand, giving it an affectionate squeeze.

James Kelly swayed and June was sure he was going to throw up everywhere.

June nodded. "Sure. How'd you end up with him?"

She grinned and laughed, but didn't answer. She released James Kelly and his head dipped dangerously; June thought he would land in the mud but he put out a hand to hold himself up.

"Have fun," Maeve advised, eyes sparkling as she glided away, looking like a leaf on the wind.

June approached the vampire and studied him for a moment. He couldn't be angry with him, not when he'd known from the start that this wouldn't be the sort of gathering where James Kelly could be comfortable. He'd known and had asked him to come anyway, then gotten upset when James Kelly had done exactly what June had expected of him. "Hey."

James Kelly looked up blearily at him. He must have found the drinks before he could leave or maybe Maeve had been plying him with drinks the whole time. "Hi."

June asked, "Are you still mad at me?"

"No."

June put an around him and pulled him to his feet. "Come on, then, you can sleep it off."

"Hmm."

June brought him back to the dais and deposited him next to Kaveon. James Kelly groaned and Kaveon opened one eye.

"Oh, you found him," the other demon said.

"I did."

"I kind of hoped you wouldn't."

James Kelly curled up on his side into a ball. He'd be aching in the morning for sure.

Kaveon sat up all the way and pulled June down onto the dais. June allowed it and put an arm over James Kelly, if only to make sure that if he did try to wander off in the night, June would be aware.

MARCH 20, 1954.

Morning passed them over and by the time they woke, the other revelers had mostly cleared out. A few stragglers wandered around, trying to pick their clothes out of the trees.

June had to chase down one scamp to get his boots back and after that, he nudged the other two awake.

Kaveon stretched and yawned luxuriously. A hard jolt of yearning lanced through June's gut and brought his mind back to the bed they'd shared, once again thinking of a relationship that had been dead for years.

James Kelly sat up, frowned at both of them, then crawled to the edge of the dais and threw up.

June grimaced, watched for a bit, then went over to rub his back. "Better not to hold anything back."

James Kelly emptied his stomach, retching and moaning, then collapsed on to his side.

"How much did you drink?" June demanded.

Instead of answering, James Kelly moaned and heaved, pressing a fist to his mouth.

"Poor thing."

"I'm sorry."

June soothed, "Everyone's been there."

"No, I mean, I'm sorry."

June sat beside him and picked at the pine needles. "I didn't mean what I said."

"I didn't either."

"Yes, well, you were drunk, at least, I was just being mean."

The vampire let out a long, groaning sigh. "I barely drank."

"Were you drinking with Maeve?"

"A few glasses of wine."

June nodded and rubbed his arm. "Fairy wine is strong. Are you ready to go? Get some sleep in a real bed?"

"Please."

June reached over and shook Kaveon again. "Do you need a ride?"

"Please and thank you."

The three of them braved the woods to scrub up quickly, sluicing water over themselves, the chill helping June and Kaveon wake up more, though it set James Kelly's teeth to chattering. June shrugged off his jacket and threw it around the vampire's shoulders.

"We've got a long walk in front of us, that should warm you up," June promised.

It didn't.

An hour's trek down the mountain brought them back to the Rambler and by the end of it, James Kelly was sweaty and shaking. Everything he said came out through gritted teeth and June left him alone.

He brought Kaveon to the bus station, which was where he'd requested to be taken, but the other demon hesitated.

Kaveon rubbed the back of his neck. "I don't know where to go."

Come home with me, June wanted to offer, but he wasn't going home. "Go back to Schenectady."

"You think?"

"Figure out what's got Liz bent out of shape, really. You picked her for a reason."

Kaveon let out a long sigh and ran his hand through his curls, setting them askew. "If you say so."

"You better have," June told him. "I'll give you a ring when I get home, though. Check in."

"Thanks, Junie, you always were the best." Kaveon gave him a hug, a long one. "I've missed you, you know."

"You too."

Kaveon stepped away, then scampered back and pressed a kiss to June's mouth. He danced away, laughing as he went.

James Kelly didn't seem to have noticed. He was buried beneath June's jacket still and when June brought him to a motel, he went right to bed.

June rummaged through his suitcase to see if he'd brought the right herbs for a hangover remedy. He hadn't, so he settled on making James Kelly drink some water.

While the vampire slept it off, June took the chance to reorganize his suitcase and then take a long bath.

The following morning, though, James Kelly didn't seem much improved. A day of sleep should have cured him.

June perched on the bed next to him around three in the afternoon. "Hey."

"Mm."

"Are you, uh. Do you need anything?"

"No. Do you?"

June raised an eyebrow. "Uh. No. Thanks."

"I'm sorry I was so awful to you."

"You weren't."

James Kelly pushed himself up. "I was. I shouldn't treat you like that, you're so good to me."

June squirmed. He didn't want his praises sung and especially not while James Kelly was unwell.

"It was just...you know, I want to do so much and then I freeze up. I think too much and there were so many people. I'm sorry. I am." The vampire started to sniffle. His voice came out small and choked. "There's things I can't do no matter how much I try."

"Oh, well. You know. You're. It's all new."

James Kelly rubbed his eyes.

"Lay back down."

He did.

"You probably just need some more sleep, I bet."

"I love you."

June smiled and patted his shoulder. "I love you, too."

"I don't…"

"Shh."

James Kelly stopped.

"Close your eyes. Go to sleep." June pulled the covers up some more, tucking him in. "I've got to eat something but…"

James Kelly had already fallen asleep and June figured he must have been really exhausted.

The second morning, James Kelly was up before June, moving around the motel room, humming dreamily to himself. He brought June a cup of coffee and kissed him. "Good morning."

June took the coffee, frowning. "Morning."

"What's wrong?"

"I thought you were sick."

A smile broke on James Kelly's face, soft and calm. "Oh. No. I feel better."

He looked a little shaky still, but his mood had improved a lot. June sipped his coffee and watched as James Kelly got all their things in order.

When he got into the shower, James Kelly came in with him and had his hands absolutely all over June. At first, June didn't have the presence of mind to complain, but when James Kelly started to kiss him deeply, June found himself a little confused.

"Uh." June cleared his throat.

"What's wrong?"

"Nothing, just, uh." There wasn't an appropriate way to remind James Kelly that they'd long since agreed that showers were for getting clean and not for petting. "You know, are you sure about this?"

"Of course." The vampire continued on with an oddly dreamy kind of urgency, like he wasn't sure what he was doing but knew he needed to do it.

June stopped him once he started to kneel. "Don't. Come on, stand up. Let's get washed up."

Wounded, James Kelly complied.

June nestled his hand against the vampire's cheek. "Don't be sore about it, kid, I just…"

"You like your showers, I know. I'm sorry."

"No need for sorry," June assured and gave him a gentle kiss. "Let me wash your back, huh?"

The vampire nodded.

Helping each other wash up had a calm, quiet intimacy that June appreciated, sometimes more than he appreciated anything involving the several varieties of penetration available to two like-minded men.

June, however, ended up rebuffing James Kelly's advances again as they started to get dressed and June had to ask, "What's gotten into you?"

He didn't think he'd ever want James Kelly to touch him less, but there was something on the other man's face that was not quite right. Maybe he still wasn't feeling well, or maybe he was out of it from too much sleep. Maybe he needed blood. June didn't know but he felt unsettled by the disconnect between James Kelly's eager hands and confused face.

"I...I just want to make you happy."

"I am happy," June told him.

"Are you sure?"

"Yes, of course. Let's just...you know, get some breakfast."

James Kelly nodded and got to it, moving with the same eagerness he'd had in the shower. He packed up everything and brought all their suitcases out to the Rambler before June had even finished dressing.

When June made it outside, James Kelly was waiting by the car, a nervous smile on his face. "I got everything ready."

"Thanks."

James Kelly beamed at him.

June frowned.

"What, what's wrong?" the vampire asked right away.

"Nothing, nothing. How do you feel?"

"I...Uh. I feel fine. Sort of...nervous, maybe, but...I'm fine."

"No more headache?" June asked.

"No."

June nodded. "That's good at least."

He wanted to put his arm around the other man and press a kiss to his temple but didn't. He climbed inside the Rambler and barely hid his surprise when James Kelly followed him inside the convenience store to scrounge up something for breakfast. He desperately wanted to go home, to sleep in his own bed and make a meal for himself.

"You hungry?"

"No, I just wanted to spend time with you," James Kelly replied.

The clerk gave James Kelly a look.

"Oh." June browsed through the aisle, recalling a time when food hadn't come in packages or cans.

He settled, eventually, on a bag of Pepperidge Farms cookies and another coffee. He approached the counter to ask for cigarettes, James Kelly on his heels, the clerk still giving them a look. He rang them out with a scowl on his face.

The clerk grumbled something under his breath as he tossed June's cigarettes on the counter and James Kelly asked, "What was that?"

June froze in the middle of counting out the right coins.

The clerk glared.

"No, go on, say it so I can hear it," the vampire challenged.

June dropped the whole handful of coins on the counter, grabbed his purchases, and hauled James Kelly out, hissing, "What's gotten into you!"

"I thought you didn't want me to be afraid."

"Well, no, of course I don't," June assured, then added, "But, kid, I'd like to make it out of town with all my teeth in my head."

A look of unease passed over James Kelly's face.

"Come on, before he follows us out or something." June pushed him towards the car, feeling bad for manhandling him, but he wanted this coffee more than he wanted to get in a fight.

"Are you mad at me?"

"No."

They didn't speak again until they were out of town and then James Kelly repeated, "Are you mad at me?"

"No. Why do you keep asking me that?"

With earnestness and more than a little apprehension, James Kelly insisted, "I don't want you to be mad at me."

"I'm not mad at you. I'm almost never mad at you and...you know, I don't even get mad when you deserve it," June reminded.

The vampire pressed his lips together and nodded. He stayed quiet for a few minutes, then asked, "Where are we going?"

"Lake George. Well, not that far east but pretty close. Last stop before we can go fucking *home*."

"Oh."

June didn't know what else to say so he focused on not spilling or burning himself on his coffee.

James Kelly offered, "Do you want me to drive?"

"No, I'm alright."

"Are you sure?"

"Yes," June said with a nod and glance in the vampire's direction. "Are you *sure* you feel alright?"

The vampire nodded.

June didn't think he was lying, but he also didn't think that he was alright. Maybe he had a fever or maybe he felt guilty about shouting at June. Or about sucking on Maeve's fingers, whatever that had been about. He didn't press the issue, though.

June headed south, following the signs for Lake George, and tried to enjoy the view as they went. The scenes framed by his windows and windshield were all absolutely picturesque, each one of them worthy of a postcard.

James Kelly watched him the entire time.

"Look out the window, why don't you?"

James Kelly looked out the window.

When they got to the Tottenham dairy farm, June suggested that he go look at the cows and he went, even though June didn't think he had liked the cows very much at the first two dairy farms.

After he'd tended to the livestock, June found James Kelly staring out at the pastures, his eyes fixed on the grazing herds.

"Shit, have you blinked at all?"

James Kelly looked over, neither amused nor irritated. "Yes."

"What are you doing?"

"What you told me to do."

"Uh." June shifted and scratched the side of his nose. He looked over James Kelly and let out a sigh.

"Are you—"

"No!" June snapped.

James Kelly hesitated, chewed his lip, then asked in a voice hardly more than a whisper, "Are you angry?"

"Why do you keep asking me that!"

"Because I don't want you to be mad at me!" he cried, his face scrunching.

"But I'm *never* mad at you, why...I mean, what's got you thinking that I'm gonna start being mad now?" June pressed.

James Kelly rubbed his face with his hands. "I don't *know*." Distress crept into his tone, making it high and desperate.

"What do you mean?"

"I mean...I mean it's just *really important*, alright, I really don't want you to be mad at me. I want to make you happy."

June rubbed his nose and studied him for a minute. This was definitely wrong, no two ways about it, and it was more than the aftermath of jealousy and fighting. "Why?" he asked, no idea what he would get for an answer.

"Because I have to."

That had not been anything close to what June had expected. "You haven't."

"I do, June. I do, I need to make you happy."

Shifting and afraid to know the answer, June opened his mouth to ask what had happened in the woods with Maeve, then considered that out in the open might not be the best place to have this discussion. He decided to table the discussion for a while. Maybe this would go away.

June nodded towards the car. "Come on, hon, let's go."

James Kelly followed him, that ecstatically happy smile back on his face over nothing more than a fond manner of being addressed.

June prayed this would go away.

MARCH 24, 1954.

June tried to give it time, but James Kelly didn't seem any better. He followed June around and asked incessantly if he needed anything; if he wasn't doing that, he was in a dreamy haze, somewhere between a stupor and being lost.

"Come sit down."

James Kelly stopped staring out the window, which he'd been doing for half an hour, and sat across from June at the small table in their motel room. They'd been here for a few days, giving June a break from driving and James Kelly some time to come back to his senses.

"What happened with Maeve?"

With a shrug, the vampire replied, "I had a few drinks. We talked a little."

"I mean in the woods."

The vampire frowned. "In the woods?"

"After we fought, I found you with her out there. In the stream."

"I..." James Kelly shook his head.

"Think," June pressed.

"I don't know what you're talking about."

"Dammit, you had her fingers in your mouth!"

James Kelly flinched at June's raised voice. "I'm sorry, I don't know, don't be angry."

June sighed. "I'm not."

"Please."

June assured him, "I'm not. But I need you to think. Really hard. What did she say to you, did she offer you anything?"

James Kelly shook his head. "I really don't know. I don't remember anything. Just...you know, being awful to you and then we were in the woods. I don't..."

June took his hand. "Please, try your hardest, think. It would make me happy."

Gripping June's hand, James Kelly bit his lip and screwed up his face, looking like he was trying to bend the walls with his mind. "I can't," he whispered.

"Please." June tightened his hold on the vampire's hand. "For me."

James Kelly nodded his head and closed his eyes tight.

Cold seeped into June's gut when he saw a trickle of blood ooze from James Kelly's nose. "Stop, stop."

James Kelly crumpled in on himself, sniffling and shaking. He didn't seem to even notice that he'd started to bleed. "I'm sorry, I'm so sorry, I don't know."

June left his chair to crouch beside him. "Hey, it's alright. I'm sorry, that was stupid of me." He cradled James Kelly's cheek with one hand. "We'll figure it out."

"I'm sorry."

"You're fine." June fished out a handkerchief and dabbed under James Kelly's nose, relieved to see that the bleeding had already stopped.

"I'm so sorry." The vampire started to cry, falling into June's arms, weeping apologies over and over.

June locked his arms around him, rocking him, hoping to do anything that could make him feel better. He kissed his temple. "Shh, alright, you haven't got to worry. We'll go home and I'll, uh, I'll make some calls, alright. See if we can't get this sorted."

"I tried."

"I know."

The first step, really, was to know what had happened between him and Maeve, or if this was her doing at all. Who knew what James Kelly had gotten up to unattended in the woods? It had been a festival night and a full moon, and Maeve had not been the only fairy around. Nothing could be done until that bit was unraveled.

James Kelly snaked his arms around June and crawled onto his lap. "I'm sorry, I am, let me make it up to you."

"You haven't—"

The vampire kissed him, hard and insistent. "You can do anything you want to me."

It was an appalling offer, his face streaked with tears and his eyes swollen. It wasn't a sultry promise, either, but one that rang of desperation, the bargain a mother might make to protect her child.

"I don't—"

James Kelly swallowed up his words with a kiss, sliding his tongue into June's mouth and rolling his hips. "You can fuck me."

"I don't want to fuck you!" June exclaimed. "I mean...you know, not like this, not when you've got—"

James Kelly tried to kiss him again, his hands working to undo June's pants.

June grabbed him by the wrists. "Stop that, really."

He went still. "I..."

"No, don't be sorry, alright? Don't ask if I'm mad. We'll just...things are a little muddled, you know, I don't want to do anything we'll regret."

"I won't regret it."

"I will," June informed him. "So don't."

"At all?"

"Not until we've figured out what's happened to you, okay? You've...I mean, shit, you're missing time, which is never good."

"I just want to make you happy."

June nodded. He'd expected the response. "What about you? What if I want to make you happy? What would make you happy right now?"

"I...I..." James Kelly licked his lips. "Listening to you makes me happy. Tell me what to do."

June began to realize how bad it was. He touched his forehead to James Kelly's and rubbed his back. "We'll be alright," he promised, even though James Kelly hadn't indicated that he wanted any kind of reassurance. "Let's...let's get home, first, okay?"

"Okay."

June didn't really think home would be helpful, but at least it would be somewhere familiar. At least at home, he had people he could talk to about this.

The drive home was more of this new, strange James Kelly, desperate to please and, June realized, terrified of making him angry. It didn't seem to be a fear based in anticipation of physical retaliation, he didn't flinch or throw up his hands, but some kind of deep and abiding nervousness, something that careened wildly past anxiety to the point where June worried that James Kelly might hurt himself.

June tried to balance it out, letting him help with small things, like getting the door or lighting a cigarette for him. Little acts like that seemed to bring him joy and to keep him from trying to do more.

"Will you get the bags?" June asked when they finally arrived home.

James Kelly narrowly missed being hit by a car in his haste to obey and June had to stop himself from screaming at him to be careful. Instead, he thanked him and got a huge smile in return.

Wei, when he saw them, got up from the couch and scolded, "You're late, y'know."

June rolled his eyes. "And?"

"You take me for granted, Junius Thompson, finkin you can wander in *two days late* like I've not been worried."

James Kelly scowled at Wei.

"I tried to call."

Wei cracked a smile. "I know, Andrew told me, I was just givin ya a hard time. Oh, you look proper knackered though. Long trip?"

June nodded.

"I'll be out of yer hair then. Oh! This woman kept callin, somefink about that one." He nodded towards James Kelly. "Lizabef or somefink."

"Thanks. I owe you."

"You do."

June gave Wei a hug and sent him on his way, wondering how

many nights of babysitting or free contraceptive services Wei would feel entitled too after so many extra nights of apartment sitting.

Gordon hurried up to June and started to wind around his ankles, yowling and purring. June crouched down to pet him properly and felt bad, as he always did, for leaving him for so long.

James Kelly had disappeared into the bedroom and when June peeked in, saw him at work unpacking the suitcases, sorting out everything that needed to be washed or hung.

June decided to leave him alone, knowing that interrupting him would only make James Kelly think he'd done something wrong.

He studied the phone for a solid five minutes, trying to work up the nerve to call back Elizabeth, not knowing what he would tell her or if he should have James Kelly talk to her in his current state.

Better to do it now, he decided, and picked up the phone. He would call them, tell them James Kelly had a stomach bug or something, then see if he could manage to mediate any of this with a brew of his own.

He had confidence in his ability to make teas for menstrual cramps or morning sickness, to weave a spell for easing labor pains or helping a barren plot of land bear fruit, but he didn't have a lot of experience outside of the realm of fertility. Hangover cures and little spells for conjuring light or unlocking doors were all that he'd ever managed to master.

He told Harold that James Kelly wasn't feeling well, but that he'd call when he was; Harold took the news quietly and with few questions, not wondering how a vampire would get a stomach bug. His words with June were terse and June suspected it had something to do with how little they had seen of their son lately.

James Kelly had avoided them when he'd been with Anastasia, too. June wondered if Elizabeth had been trying to set him up with other women then, too, or if he'd avoided them because he'd had his condition so poorly managed.

After the call, he settled into the couch with a general spell book and Gordon on his lap.

James Kelly found him that way. "I unpacked everything."

"Thank you."

He smiled so broadly, with such unrestrained joy, that June

wanted to kiss him. "What are you reading?"

"Uh. Just some spells."

His pale gold eyes narrowed for half a second. "About…about the way I am now?"

Even cursed or bewitched or whatever he was, he was still sharp. June didn't think there would be much point in lying to him. "Yes."

"You don't like me like this, do you?"

"I worry."

James Kelly's hands balled into fists and June thought he would see some of that anger spark through, a little bit of his usual defiance, but his hands relaxed in an instant. "I…I can't stop."

"What do you mean?"

"It's like…I know what I'm doing, I know it's…" James Kelly rubbed his face. "I know it's not how I normally am. I *know* something is different, but I can't control it."

June thought it would have been better if he hadn't. If he could have been blissfully unaware, if his real self hadn't been in there with him, watching all this miserable subservience. "You can come sit with me if you like."

He nodded, then came over, curling up beside June. He rested his head against June's arm. "I…"

"What?"

Quietly, he admitted, "June, I'm worried."

"Things will be alright."

"If you don't like me like this how can I make you happy?"

"I like you," June whispered past the lump in his throat. "You make me happy just by being here."

The vampire shook his head. "It's not enough."

June put an arm around him and pulled him in closer, pressing a kiss to his temple. "James Kelly, I love you. You're what makes me happy," he insisted but the other man seemed to take no comfort in it. "I'm going to go on reading. You could read, too."

James Kelly nodded, fetched a book, which was not the one he'd been reading before, just the first one he came across, but he settled in next to June with it. Gordon stretched himself out across the back of the couch and James Kelly even reached up to pet him once.

It felt normal, sitting together like that, and June was almost able to pretend that nothing had happened. It gave him a little bit of hope that maybe if this couldn't be fixed, it could at least be managed.

The next day he tried the first promising brew he'd come across, putting on the radio like he usually did when he worked.

James Kelly watched him, a weirdly blank expression of anxiety on his face.

"Why don't you do a crossword puzzle?" June suggested after he could no longer stand to be watched any longer. Grinding herbs into a paste was not interesting and should not have garnered anyone's attention for this long.

"Uh."

"Go on," June said.

"Is...is that what you want me to do?"

"I'd be pleased as punch."

James Kelly nodded and headed to the kitchen table, taking up the newspaper and a pen. He worked quietly for a while and June returned his attention to the herbs until he became aware of a quiet, keening noise behind him. He turned away from the stove, dreading whatever he would see.

Rigid but shaking, James Kelly had his pen poised above the newspaper. He'd gone gray and the sounds that escaped him reminded June of what it sounded like when someone tried to stitch their own wounds shut.

"What's wrong?"

"I can't do this one," James Kelly whispered, his voice trembling. "I don't know the answer. I can't do it."

"Oh, well...um. Maybe you should take a break."

He shook his head. "No, if you want me to finish it then I will."

"I've got something else for you to do now."

His eyes snapped to June's, relief breaking over his face, making June wonder how long he had been stuck on that one word.

June finished up the brew and brought it over to him, clearing the crossword from the table. "Here, drink thi—not yet!" He shot out his hand to stop James Kelly from bringing it directly to his lips. "Wait a bit, it's hot."

"What's it for?"

"Remembering."

"Oh."

James Kelly had his hands wrapped around the mug and June slid his hands on top of his. It was a normal feeling moment and June had started to savor those. He'd spent about an hour last night watching the vampire sleep because it had been the only time when he had looked himself.

June took his hands back and warned, "It's going to taste awful."

"Everything..."

"What?"

James Kelly shook his head. "It wouldn't have been nice."

"Go on, tell me."

A clear struggle played out on his features, but eventually, the vampire whispered, "Everything you make tastes awful."

June beamed. "I know, it's medicine, it's not supposed to taste good."

James Kelly brought the mug to his lips, wincing at the taste. "Have I got to drink all of it?"

"Please. But take your time."

When the mug had been emptied, James Kelly dutifully brought it over to the sink and washed it. June made sure to thank him.

"How will I know if it's working?"

"It'll take about half an hour to kick in. You'll, well, hmm." June took up the spell book again and read, "The book describes it as feeling an increased clarity regarding and awareness of past events in your life."

He nodded.

June skimmed the passage once more, checking for side effects, which were limited to increased heart rate and minor headaches. He shuddered to think what sort of things this potion would have him remembering if he'd been the one to take it and, with a jolt of unease, recalled all the unpleasant things that James Kelly must have tried to forget about.

Hopefully, the recollections would be navigable.

They settled onto the couch together and June eyed the clock for the next thirty minutes, asking if James Kelly had remembered anything every so often. It must have been irritating but James Kelly didn't seem annoyed, just apologetic.

"What about now?"

"Uh. What do you want me to remember?" James Kelly asked.

"Think back to the festival."

He nodded.

"What happened?"

James Kelly closed his eyes and almost as if he were reading from a passage, told June, "We had walked up the mountain for about an hour or so. If I look up I can see all the stars and I've never seen so many stars in all my life. You point up and you tell me that it's the Milky Way that's going across the sky. There's people a little ways behind us, I can hear them cracking twigs as they walk. Three of them—"

"Good, good. Now, uh. You remember us arguing?"

He nodded. "You'd been dancing with Kaveon around the fire and everyone dancing around you started to—"

"You walked away, where did you go after you walked away?"

"I...I walked away and I was headed towards the woods, I was going to, I don't know what I was going to do, I didn't even know then. I had to get away, though, because I felt sick to my stomach and I couldn't think straight. I couldn't believe that I'd...June, your face when I said that! You looked like I'd—"

June had no interest in knowing how his face had looked in that moment. "What happened?"

"I was going to walk back to the car," the vampire said.

"And?"

"And...I started to. But I wasn't paying attention, I walked out of the clearing but not on to the path. I thought I heard my name..."

"Go on."

James Kelly shook his head. "That's it."

June wanted to press him for answers but recalled the nosebleed he'd gotten last time. "You're sure?" he asked, unable to help himself.

"Yes. That's all. After I leave the path I can't remember anything."

"Sure."

"And then you were there. In the stream."

June nodded and gave the other man's thigh a pat. "That's alright."

"You had this look on your face."

"No, that's alright. You don't have to keep thinking about that now."

"What should I think about?"

With an easy shrug, June said, "Anything you like!"

The vampire started to fidget. After a few minutes, his fidgeting turned to outright trembling. His eyes darted nervously around the room.

"What?"

He whispered, "I, uh. I can't. It's…"

"It's what?" June asked.

He buried his face in his hands, shaking. "It's so loud and the plane, it's…I can't, I can't. It's like they're screaming."

June didn't know much about his time in the army, but he knew that had involved shooting down planes. It was the only detail James Kelly ever shared and, to June's knowledge, the only time he'd ever been involved with planes. It didn't seem like the kind of thing for which one would want increased clarity and awareness.

He clamped his arms around James Kelly, hauling him closer. "Think about something else, think about something good."

"I can't."

"Do you remember that baseball game!" June urged, his own voice cracking a little. "We went to see the Dodgers on opening day. Don't you remember that? We had a great time, back to back wins, wasn't it? And we walked home and you kept talking about the game. Going on about the crack of the bat."

"I remember."

"Tell me about that. Tell me about the baseball game."

"It was April," he started, his voice thick. "You were wearing a suit. Gray flannel wool and a blue tie. I keep sneaking glances at you and I know you saw me. But you look so good in a suit. You look good in everything. I…that morning, when you were getting dressed, you hadn't closed the door all the way and I caught a glimpse, just for a second, but I wanted to look. It was like the first time you see a dirty picture."

June grinned and nuzzled his throat. "Keep going."

He leaned into June's arms, calmer now, his voice evening out as he went on. He retold the whole day in glowing detail. Even once the brew had worn off, James Kelly didn't want to broach the topic of planes and what he'd been remembering; June didn't press it. All he did was kiss his hair and tell him that they would figure this out soon.

June hadn't had the nerve to risk another spell, not when the last one had nearly sent James Kelly into a panic. He knew he needed to do something but now he feared making things worse. He poured over all the books about memory and remembering he could borrow, cagily asking friends for their volumes and giving weak answers when they wanted to know why.

Just about everything he could find gave plenty of advice for fanning the flames of a fading memory or of how to figure out what had happened during a night of blackout drinking; he found spells for remembering important events and finding things that had been misplaced. Nothing seemed to mesh with the empty spot in James Kelly's memory. Every last book advised that if fairies were involved it was better to leave things alone and give thanks that nothing worse had happened.

It felt unacceptable.

James Kelly set a coffee in front of him on the kitchen table.

"Thank you."

The vampire beamed. It felt like a normal moment until James Kelly asked, "Can I do anything else for you?"

He'd been asking that question a lot and June didn't particularly like the way he asked it. It was coquettish and came out of the blue; this not at all the way he usually went about propositioning June.

"No."

James Kelly frowned, then bit his lip.

"It isn't you."

"Do you not—"

"It isn't anything about you," June told him. "It feels like taking advantage is all. That isn't how I want things to be between us. You've got to understand that."

"I want to make you happy."

"I'd be absolutely miserable if once we get all this sorted you felt like I'd used you. I'd rather not risk it."

He didn't seem pleased.

"What if things were the other way around? What if it were me in your shoes?" June asked since the vampire no longer seemed to have much of a grasp on his own emotions and sense of risk. "Or what if you're only focused on me because I was the first person you saw? What if it had been any person wandering around who'd come across you? You wouldn't want that, would you?"

"I." He put his hands on his hips. "No. I suppose you're right."

"Thank you for understanding."

He nodded and took half a step forward. "I would like to give you a kiss, though. And I think, uh, I think it's just me wanting it."

That was how he'd started to refer to the handful of things he wanted outside the context of making June happy, things like blood and Tootsie Rolls.

"I guess I can't say no to that."

James Kelly slid closer to him and leaned in to give him a kiss, his mouth warm and gentle until it wasn't, until he grew insistent, pushing June's chair back and settling onto his lap. June should have pulled back, but it was a wonderful kiss and they had done this so many times, though not exactly like this.

He pulled back eventually and put his forehead against the vampire's chest. "Maybe we shouldn't," he said into James Kelly's shirt. "Maybe we shouldn't get too excited. You understand, you've got to."

James Kelly was saved from having to answer or be disappointed or ask one of his sad-eyed questions by a knock at the door.

"Could you get that for me?"

"Sure!"

He seemed just as happy to do small things like that and climbed off June's lap, moving to the door with purpose.

When he was out of sight, June folded his arms on the table and buried his face in them. He couldn't keep this up for long. Something had to give and June figured it would probably be his ability to keep saying no.

"Momma? Dad?" came the vampire's voice, somewhere between confusion and irritation.

June groaned and eyed the window. It led to the fire escape and he'd used it to make a quick exit before. It didn't seem appropriate, though, so he forced himself to his feet and out to the living room.

Harold had cold, critical eyes fixed on his son and Elizabeth had the back of her hand against his forehead. "We thought you were sick," she said, adjusting the paper bag in her arm.

"No, I..." James Kelly glanced towards June.

"He's...He's not been feeling himself," June told them.

"We were *worried*," Elizabeth scolded and June got the feeling that it was direct towards him and not her son.

"Didn't know what had happened," Harold added.

To James Kelly, his mother reminded, "You were supposed to come over for dinner."

James Kelly shook his head. "I don't want to come over for dinner. I don't want to meet any of those girls."

June dragged a hand through his hair and looked around for a cigarette. He snatched up the pack as soon as he saw it.

"They're nice girls," his mother insisted.

"It wouldn't make June happy," James Kelly answered.

June coughed on his drag and cried, "I didn't! I didn't say that, don't go telling them that."

James Kelly turned to June, baffled. "Would...would it make you happy? If I went to meet them?"

"No, but—"

"I'll do it if you want me to," he offered eagerly.

Harold and Elizabeth exchanged looks of intense discomfort.

"Mouse," his mother began, gracing her son with a look that

was the epitome of caring concern.

"What's in the bag? Why don't you come in out of the doorway?" June offered, trying to be politely but coming off as overbearing and nervous.

James Kelly herded his parents inside before they'd had a chance to consent. "Do you want me to make them coffee, too?"

"Ask them."

"Do you want me to make you coffee?"

"We brought you soup, we thought you were sick," his mother said.

He asked again, "Do you want me to make you coffee?"

June sighed and tried not to intervene, finishing off a cigarette and trying to light another one. Maybe if he stayed quiet, James Kelly would forget about him for a little bit.

"No, I don't want any coffee. Thank you," she said.

"Are you sure?" James Kelly pressed.

"It's fine. Thanks for asking them," June murmured.

James Kelly looked towards him and immediately came over to light his cigarette for him.

"Thanks."

The vampire beamed, not paying an ounce of attention to his parents. "Do you need anything—"

"No, no, I'm fine. Thanks. Listen, your folks came all the way over," June said, gesturing towards them. "Why don't you spend some time with them?"

"Uh. Alright."

He went back over to his parents and sat with them, but kept sending June desperate glances until June took pity and came over to sit with them. James Kelly barely answered his parents' questions and kept asking June if he was mad or if he needed anything.

Harold grew colder and shorter with his son, until finally, he demanded, "What exactly is going on here? What is this?"

Elizabeth hissed, "Harold."

"No, this isn't right! *This* isn't how he should be. Something else is going on here," the man insisted, standing up and jabbing a finger at June.

James Kelly stood up too, angling himself towards his father.

June got to his feet, putting a hand on the vampire's chest.

"Relax, alright. Your dad's upset, give him a minute to adjust," he suggested, his voice low and mild.

Harold demanded, "What have you done to him?"

"Nothing."

"You have, this isn't right. There's something...something queer going on."

June bit his tongue to keep from telling him that what was going on was very queer indeed.

"Your sort, I know what they do. You've *done* something to him. Brainwashed him or something," Harold accused.

"Harold, really," Elizabeth soothed.

"I haven't," June told him; it took real effort to keep his voice even.

"It's not right, whatever it is!"

June took in a breath. "I haven't—"

"That's *not my son!*" the man snarled. "I knew it from the first minute he brought you around that there was something else going on. Something...wrong. Unnatural. He would never in a million years start taking up with men."

"You don't understand—"

"The hell I don't!" Harold pushed June, more than just a posturing shove.

James Kelly grabbed his father and yanked him close, all rage and protectiveness, his lips peeled back to show teeth; June was terrified that he might do real harm to the man. Elizabeth cried out, clutching her hands to her chest.

Gordon bolted from the kitchen between their legs to the bedroom.

"Don't, don't hurt him, God, Jesus Christ." June rushed to pull them apart.

The vampire faltered.

"It'd make me unhappy."

He drew back.

June fished some change out of his pocket and pressed it into James Kelly's hand. "Go get me some cigarettes, alright?"

James Kelly smiled and nodded, heading out of the apartment like he hadn't been about to bloody his father a moment ago.

"Sit down," June told Harold.

Harold didn't.

"Sit down, Harold, we've got to talk," he repeated, but it was no longer a suggestion.

Harold went back to the couch and June sat on the coffee table, not sure where to begin. He sucked in a big breath and relayed some of what had happened, leaving out the fight, just saying that James Kelly had gotten lost in the wood and run into a bit of trouble.

"But I'm trying to undo it, I swear. And then he can go have dinner with Patty whoever from Chicago. Obviously, he can't go like this."

Elizabeth's eyes opened wide and June saw a lot of resemblance between them. "He told you?"

"I'm not holding him prisoner."

"No, of course not, but well, I thought he might keep things...separate," she suggested, as though June hadn't knowingly been the object of an affair a dozen times over. The level of naivete was almost sweet and he almost wanted to let her go on thinking that dirty secrets like him ever for a second thought they meant something to anyone. The urge was tempered somewhat by Elizabeth's assumption that June would tolerate being second to someone's wife; of course, he would, he just didn't like to think of himself as that desperate for affection.

"You've got it switched. It's the wife that would need to be kept in the dark, not the other way around."

They all fidgeted.

Elizabeth smoothed her skirt, then said, "You've got to understand, we want what's best for him."

"And I want something else?"

"Well..."

"If you did, if you cared about him, you wouldn't be getting him involved in all this," Harold pointed out, the first thing he'd said since James Kelly had grabbed him.

"In what? A relationship?" June asked.

"He's got a hard enough of it time as is," his mother said; it sounded more like an apology than blame.

"And you think it'd be easier for him to go on pretending he isn't how he is?"

"He never used to be like this," Harold said.

"It would be safer," Elizabeth added.

Safer, sure, except June had seen what trying to be someone else did to people. It had them sneaking around with men they didn't know, people they could barely trust, behind the backs of their wives and families. It had them drinking and doing all kinds of drugs. It had them climbing into warm baths with razor blades.

"And less embarrassing, I bet." June had had enough. "When he comes back, you should say goodbye. I'll have him call you when this mess is sorted out. You can have this conversation with him when he's in the right state of mind."

He sat across from them, no idea what else to say. He held out the pack of cigarettes to them and almost offered them coffee before he remembered that they'd already declined.

"No, thank you," Elizabeth declined.

Harold looked at him like he'd offered him something vile.

He sighed, scratched the back of his neck and confessed, "I suppose it was always going to come to this, wasn't it? Probably should have happened sooner. I don't know what he was thinking, anyway."

They glanced at each other.

"Why didn't you? Make a fuss, I mean. On New Year's."

"You haven't got any children," Elizabeth said.

"No."

"Then you can't understand. We got that letter from the Army. It felt like I'd been shot."

June thought about asking if she'd ever been shot, but he didn't. She'd been considerably less rude than her husband.

"When he came back...when he was *alive*. I don't want to lose him again." Her voice shuddered. "And I don't want him to go back to how he was when he first came back to the city. It was horrible to see him like that."

Harold put a hand on his wife's back.

"I thought if, well, if him taking up with you was the price to pay for that, so be it, but now he won't even come over, won't take my calls."

June thumbed his nose and couldn't help asking, "You don't think maybe trying to set him up with all these girls might be what's alienating him?"

"If he could just settle down. Have a family. He'd understand once he has a family of his own."

"You know he's dead, right? I mean, his body *died*. He's going to live for...centuries if he plays his cards right. You think a wife and four or five kids are going to do him good?" He shook his head, played with a cigarette before he lit it, rolling it gently between his fingers. "He thought you wouldn't care. About the two of us. I mean, he was pretty drunk when he said it, but people tend to get honest then. But I believed him. I think he believed it, too. It must be an awful disappointment, don't you think?"

"It—"

"No, don't tell me, don't say anything. But think about it, won't you? I mean, really think about what you're asking him to do when you ask him to come over and meet those girls."

Silence stretched between them, awkward and broken only here and there by the sound of the cat pattering around.

James Kelly returned. He handed over two pack of cigarettes. "I got one and then I started to come back and thought you might want two instead, I had enough change for two."

"That's perfect. Thank you."

He looked at his parents.

His mother took up the paper bag that she'd set aside. "I made you soup."

"I don't eat."

She swallowed.

"Are you staying?" he asked.

"No. We just came by to drop this off."

He nodded. He didn't say thank you or hug his mother or shake hands with his father. He closed the door behind them.

June watched the ordeal from the kitchen and then went to sit on the coffee table, not exactly sure when he'd started viewing tables as a better place for his ass than a couch or chair. He'd always been prone to perching like this. "Hey."

James Kelly turned to face him.

"You can't go around grabbing people like that."

The other man protested, "He would have clocked you."

"Probably would have. What did you plan to do about it?"

"Stop him."

"How?" June asked.

"However I had to."

"You can't," June told him. "You can't hurt people."

The vampire pressed his lips together. "Ever?"

"Not over nothing," June amended. "If they're trying to do something bad, you know, that's one thing, but I can take a crack across the jaw well enough."

"I don't like the idea of that."

"You looked like a vampire, snarling at him like that."

"They already know."

"And what if they hadn't though? Or what if it hadn't been your parents? Creatures are supposed to keep a low profile, it's how we stay safe. Keeping us under the radar is part of my job, you know."

"I know," he replied sulkily. "You aren't mad, are you?"

"No."

James Kelly shifted and uneasily eyed the cigarette in June's hand as he brought it to his mouth for a drag.

June waved him over; the vampire sat hesitantly beside him on the coffee table and June offered the cigarette to him once he'd had his drag. Instead of slipping it out of June's fingers, he leaned in and took his hit while June still held it. He nestled his way under June's arm.

It was too bad that relations between fairies and demons had gone so sour. Maybe his relationship with Maeve wasn't as good as he'd thought. Maybe she'd done this to wound him. Too bad he didn't have a fairy to talk this out with.

The phone rang and June stretched over to answer it, dragging the whole phone back with him. He accidentally elbowed James Kelly, who returned to cuddling him.

"Hello?"

"I haven't seen you in forever," Peggy accused.

June had temporarily forgotten that anyone outside of his apartment building existed as anything other than pieces of the scenery. "Things have been...kind of strange."

"Strange how? No, don't tell me. Come over for dinner, tell me then. Tonight?"

"Uh."

"Tomorrow night then, at eight. Don't worry about bringing anything, just you and that boyfriend of yours."

"About that," he said.

"What, you aren't seeing him anymore or you were never seeing him in the first place?"

"I'm still seeing him."

"Good. I'll see you tomorrow. Marie misses you."

He sighed.

Her tone changed at that. "June, love, come on. Whatever's got you down, we'll talk about it."

The promise tempted him and a new perspective might have been exactly what he needed. "Alright, fine, don't twist my arm."

James Kelly kept trying to wind his arm around June's waist; he'd been trying to hold his hand on the subway too and June absolutely died every time he had to pull out of the other man's grasp. Without James Kelly being squirrely and tense about being in public together, it was suddenly up to June to be the vigilant one.

Things he'd never really worried about stood out to him and he realized how long it had been since he'd had anyone to be seen in public with at all. Most of his dates in the past few decades had been clandestine, at some hotel room or bar with similarly inclined men. Before that, buggery hadn't been condoned, of course, but men had been allowed to touch each other without it being suspicious.

Now that was out of the question. They'd gotten a lot of stares and whispers on the subway and more when June had needed to do damage control, assuring James Kelly that nothing was wrong, he wasn't mad, but he just needed to keep his hands to himself. Several people had moved away from them.

Once, right before they'd been set to get off, there had only been a few young men on the train. Dressed not dissimilarly to June, in tight jeans and motorcycle jackets, they'd huddled close together, their voices not as hushed as they'd thought.

One had asked, "What do you figure's wrong with the blue

one?"

"What do you figure's wrong with *both* of them?" had been the response from his friend.

"Pair of faggots, that's what," the third had said. "Geez, Rico, can't you tell anything?"

Rico had fumbled to recover, "Yeah, they're fags for sure, but I mean, shit, *look* at them, don't they look weird?"

They were an odd pair, June had to concede. A blue man with horns was an unusual enough sight for most people and to find him dressed like a greaser with a well-dressed black man practically trying to crawl into his lap on the subway must have been concerning.

Of course, June had been equally curious as to what the youths were doing on a train to the Upper East Side at just before eight on a weekday.

"You think they're up to something?" one had asked and all three had glanced towards them.

"I don't know, hey, Rico, why don't you go find out?" another had suggested, giving Rico a push and a leering smile.

Rico had pushed him back and the three had fallen to squabbling, letting June and James Kelly slip off the train unnoticed. It had been a few stops too early, but the night wasn't as cold as it had been recently and June didn't mind the walk.

June rapped on the door of Peggy's townhouse and allowed James Kelly to finally hold him. They'd be inside soon, no one else was about at the moment and it was dark anyway. The risk was minimal.

Marie answered the door, giving them her usual scowl, but it didn't reach her eyes. Her yellow dress clashed wonderfully with her pale purple skin.

"You cut your hair."

She nodded. "I did."

"You look like Jackie Coogan in a dress."

She snorted and took him by the arm. "Come on, come in."

He stepped inside, James Kelly holding his hand as he trailed behind.

"Drink?" Marie offered.

June opened his mouth to accept, then stopped and stared at her. There was something he had to say, some thought that had wandered, nascent and desperately important, through his mind. "You're a fairy."

She raised an eyebrow and waited.

"Marie!" he exclaimed, grabbing her by the shoulders. "You beautiful creature."

She wrinkled her nose and stepped out of his grasp. "What?"

"You can help, can't you? You've got magic."

Her face went blank. She shook her head and headed towards the kitchen. "Peggy ran out to pick up the food and get something to drink, she'll be back in a bit. Find a seat."

"Marie-George Durand," he called after her, "I'm not asking for party tricks or wishes, I'm asking for help."

She paused, her hand on the doorframe. She turned. "What do you need help with?"

He slung his eyes over his shoulder towards James Kelly, who had come up behind him and crept his arms around June's torso.

She studied the two of them. "Who'd he tangle with?"

"He can't remember." He stepped out of the other man's embrace.

James Kelly began, "Are you—"

"No," June cut him off.

She looked over James Kelly some more. She mussed her hair as she thought. "Alright, fine. Fine." She huffed and made a sweeping gesture for them to head into the living room. "Sit."

They did and she sat on the floor in front of them, leaning against the coffee table, her feet tucked under the couch. "Start from the beginning."

June opened his mouth.

"Not you, him."

James Kelly glanced towards June.

"Go ahead," June urged.

The vampire licked his lips and began with, "We'd fought."

"I need more than that. I need the whole thing. Go to the start. Why were you fighting, what happened before you fought?" she asked.

His fingers scrabbled against the flannel wool of his trousers and June put his hand over his, blue against brown. The vampire sucked in a breath and June wondered if he needed to breathe, if it was a reflex left over from his human life or if he'd be gasping for air if someone covered his face. He started to talk, vague at first but adding all the details Marie probed out of him.

She came to the same wall June had. He'd stepped off the path, thought he'd heard his name, and didn't remember anything after that.

"You stepped off *then* thought you'd heard your name?"

"No, the other away around."

She nodded.

June asked, "What difference does it make?"

"Means it wasn't by accident."

"Uh." June glanced at the vampire. "But why?"

"I don't know." To James Kelly, she said, "Maybe one of them took a shine to you." She cocked her head, then sat up. "I can probably get those memories out but...well, as for whatever is going on with you, I don't know about that."

James Kelly looked June's way.

"Go on."

"I..."

"What?"

"I can't say I'm keen on the idea," the vampire admitted. It was the most resistance he'd shown to anything. He tightened his hand on June's.

Understandable, June reasoned. His last encounter with fairies had gone positively sideways. "You'll be alright, huh?"

He nodded. "If it'll make you happy."

June leaned in, pressed his forehead to James Kelly's shoulder. "Please."

"Alright. Alright, fine."

Marie stood up and stretched, up on her toes, hands above her head. Her back popped a few times and she waved her hand between the two of them. "Scoot over, I need to get in here." She squeezed herself in when June didn't move fast enough for her.

She folded her legs beneath herself and reached one hand towards James Kelly's head. "I've got to touch you, you know? Would it be better if I touched you somewhere particular?"

"I don't think so."

She placed her hands on him, one on the top of his head and

one on his shoulder.

He tensed visibly.

In the kindest voice June had ever heard out of Marie, she assured, "I'm not going to hurt you, okay? Fairies can't lie."

"You're only half," the vampire reminded.

"And I'm a horrible liar."

June slid back to sit on the arm of the couch to get a better view, resting his elbows on his knees, feeling momentarily guilty for putting his boots on Peggy's couch.

The two of them were still, still as June had ever seen Marie be without being mad enough to spit. Every so often James Kelly would give a bit of a twitch or a small grunt from the back of his throat like he'd been pushed.

June chewed his nails, which had started to look more like claws again, but made the stupid idiot mistake if digging one of his fangs into a barely-healed crack and right into the bed of his nail.

He clenched up and let out all his breath as a concentrated huff through his nose. His finger started to throb and he sandwiched it hard between his knees.

When Marie took her hands from James Kelly, she sat back.

The vampire leaned forward and June thought he was going he was going to be sick; he only sucked in a few breaths and then sat up.

"Well?" June probed.

"I..."

"Do you remember anything?"

"I stepped off the path because this voice kept calling my name. I thought it was my mother and I couldn't figure what she'd be doing out here, but you know, what kind of person would I be if I didn't check? I tried to find her but the voice kept changing directions and then it changed altogether. It didn't sound like her anymore."

June wanted to press him for answers.

"It was men's voices and I thought I should get out of there. I didn't think I'd gone more than a few yards from the path but when I looked back I couldn't see it. I couldn't even see the bonfire through the trees anymore and I started to really worry. No matter what way I turned though, I ended up somewhere else. I'd set off for an oak and I'd end up near a pine. Like the forest was moving under my feet.

"And then it wasn't just voices. I could feel things, like...hands maybe, or a bramble. Like something was tugging at me, always out of sight and I'd look and I'd only catch it out of the corner of my eye. I don't know how long it was but then...then I heard her. The queen. She was in the stream, looking up at the moon. I'd tried to run, thought I'd seen the bonfire and then I was there at the bank. She told off whatever was there. I was just about set to...to you know, really lose it, I think."

Marie left the couch and went over to the bar, started rummaging around and June slid off the arm of the couch. The vampire had pallor to him and a bit of a shake in his voice and June didn't want to hear anything else. He wanted to wrap him up and take him home.

"Go on," June urged.

"She called me rude. Told me I'd been abhorrently rude to you and I said that...that I couldn't help it, which she said was a lie. Ignorance is one thing, being cruel is another. She said I'd been cruel to you. I told her that I didn't know what else to do, that I'd been...June, you were dancing with him like that and I'd wanted it to be me. You asked and I kept saying no even though I...I'm not like that, you know! I don't dance, not to that kind of music, not *wild* like you two were. You looked so happy with him. I told her I wished I could do what I had to do to make you happy."

"Those were your words?" June asked.

"Yes."

"Exactly."

"Yes."

"You said you wished?" Marie asked from the bar. She hadn't made herself a drink yet, but she'd moved about every bottle and glass at the bar.

"Yes."

June kept his face even, but it took real effort. It was worse than he'd thought. "Then what?"

"She told me she could do that for me and I was so...everything had been so strange and I just wanted to go home and be with you. I wanted things to be the way they're supposed to be! And I felt so bad about what I'd said; she was right, I was being cruel. I said yes. Then she sort of...wiped something off the air, like you'd wipe dust off a dirty window and told me that it would fix things. I...ate it. Off her fingers."

June pressed his knees harder together, sending a burst of ache through his cracked nail. "And?"

"And then you found us."

"Shit," Marie proclaimed. "This is...not good."

"There's got to be something," June said.

She reminded, "Wishes are gifts. You don't return gifts, not from the queen."

"He can't stay like this."

"I know." Marie looked over the vampire again. "Let me, uh, let me talk to my father. He might have an idea."

The door opened and they all looked over like it might be a murderer, but it was only Peggy with bags in her arms.

"I'm sorry, my goodness, have I got a story to tell you. There was this mix up at the restaurant and they were trying to give me enough food, I swear, for a family of ten!" she began, then trailed off, taking in the somber mood of the room. "What?"

"Nothing," June said. He'd tell her about it some other time, or she'd get the story from Marie.

"Have you got to put your boots on the couch, June?" Peggy asked as she headed into the kitchen. "Marie, can you come help me get plates?"

"I'm sorry." June sat normally, next to James Kelly, who leaned against him, not nuzzling or cuddling, but like he'd collapsed and June had gotten in the way of his swoon.

"June," he said, his voice a plaintive whisper.

"What?"

"I really am worried."

"We'll get this sorted," June told him.

"I shouldn't have done any of that."

"You didn't know what she was going to do, not really."

"I'm sorry I'm so awful sometimes, I know...you're so good to me, I should...I shouldn't expect you not to go looking other places when I can't give you what you want."

"You absolutely should expect that," June vowed. He drew the other man into a hug. "I was being an ass, bringing you there and expecting that you'd take to it like a fish to water. But now we know, alright? And Maeve, I think she likes me. Maybe she'll reconsider if we can find the right way to ask."

"You really think so?"

June nodded, even though he didn't think the odds of a fairy queen taking back a wish were anything more than slim on a good day. If it had been one of her courtiers making trouble, maybe she would have undone things. He kissed the vampire's temple.

They didn't talk about it anymore but when they left for the night, Marie promised to be in touch soon.

She made good on her promise the following afternoon, calling to say that her father had secured them an audience with the fairy queen. She would be by to get them tomorrow night.

"You're coming?" June asked, not able to mask his surprise.

"Better if I come with you otherwise they might not let you in without a hard time."

"They wouldn't let me in?"

"No, they'd let you in but who knows if you'd make it to the court. What are you going to bring as a gift?"

"A gift?"

"You know, it'll put her in a good mood," Marie told him. "It's optional, the same way that birthday presents are optional when your wife turns seventy."

June smirked, remembering the fiasco that had been Peggy's forgotten birthday. "Alright, I'll think of something. Any ideas?"

"She's a fairy," came the response. It was an answer that only Marie could have given, lumping them all together like that; if anyone else had said something like that, it would have been a to-do.

June didn't press it, just thanked her, and hung up.

He didn't know what a good gift for a fairy would be and he couldn't think straight with James Kelly around, asking if he needed something, if he was mad, if there was anything he wanted. It wasn't just the interruptions, it was the ever-present sense of dread June got whenever he looked at him. He couldn't stay this way and it wasn't just June's preference.

Their relationship had gone from mutual to obligation in a

single night because now June would never be able to break things off with him. It was his fault all this had happened and he didn't even want to think how this new James Kelly would take a break up.

He didn't want to think about how the real James Kelly, the one who still peeked out from time to time, would take it either.

And he didn't even want to break up with him! He didn't know how he'd gotten onto that train of thought. They weren't going to break up, they were going to get things sorted out.

Somehow.

If June could find a way to think.

"Are you mad?"

"No."

"Is there anything I can do?"

"No."

James Kelly pressed his lips together and looked at his hands, squeezing the thumb on one hand.

"Actually."

The vampire looked up right away.

"Can you..."

James Kelly waited eagerly, his eyes on June's face like a child waiting for a present.

"Can you go get me...uh. A pack of cigarettes?"

"Sure."

"But, um, not from the store down the street, can you, um, you know that store in Chinatown, right next to the noodle place?" June asked.

"Yes."

"Can you go there and get them?"

"Sure. Do you want noodles?" James Kelly asked, starting to show a bit of puzzlement.

"No. Walk there."

The vampire didn't protest, he said, "Sure," but June thought he saw a glimmer of thought behind the vampire's eyes.

June rooted around in the bowl where he tossed his keys and loose change and plucked out a dollar in quarters. "And, you know, get yourself something if you want it. A candy bar or a newspaper or something."

"Sure." James Kelly took the quarters and dropped them into

his pocket. "Anything else?"

"Be safe. Watch out for cars."

The vampire nodded and June thought he saw a bit of a flush across his cheeks and ears. The other day he'd walked right out into traffic without the slightest hesitance and June had just about had a heart attack.

Before he could leave, June caught him by the arm and pulled him in for a hug. "I love you."

"I love you, too."

June watched him go and tried to wrack his brain for something that would please Maeve. He didn't think anything from Earth would do and even if there was something here that she'd want, he didn't have the money for it. The whole of Tiffany's might not have pleased her when it came to the baubles the human world had to offer.

He needed something splendid and unique and thrilling. If he'd been even halfway decent with spells for anything but encouraging sprouts, he could have made her something; if he'd even had more time, he could have found a mage and bought something from them.

He could have gotten her a baby, fairies were always after human babies for some reason, but kidnapping babies was a moral horizon he wasn't ready to breach, not even for James Kelly.

He needed help; he needed someone who was unique and splendid and thrilling to give him an idea.

He needed...Of course. He needed his king.

The prayer came to his lips, an easy and desperate supplication. "I need you, please."

There was no sound or scent or stirring of air to announce his arrival, but something about the feel of the room changed and June opened his eyes to find his king, naked and sopping wet, standing in his kitchen.

"What?"

June grinned.

"What, what is it?" the Devil demanded.

"I just...I need a favor," he admitted, a little sheepish.

"Christ, Junius, I thought something was wrong!"

"Were you in the bath?"

"Yes, I was," Lucifer told him. He jabbed a finger June's direction. "And I was having a lot of fun, too. Give me one reason I shouldn't go back."

June felt his grin widen. "Because you're going to do me a favor."

"Get me a towel."

June fetched a towel and a bathrobe, handing them both over.

"You didn't even bow or anything," the Devil sulked.

A vision of him sinking to his knees before him, no more than a few inches from the Devil's skin, came into June's head; it must have shown on his face, because Lucifer cleared his throat and pulled on the robe, cinching it about his waist.

"Well, what do you need?" he demanded.

June drew in a breath and explained the situation as simply as he could, knowing there wasn't a lot of time to waste.

By the time it had been told, Lucifer had wrung out his hair and fixed it into a thick plait. "It is best to let fairies deal with fairy business...I'd offer to speak with her on your behalf but, uh, I'm afraid Maeve doesn't like me much. If it was that king, for the other court, that'd be different. He and I have managed to work out a few things. Anyways. You need a gift."

June nodded. "Please."

"Fine. This is why everyone thinks you're my favorite."

"I am your favorite."

Lucifer grinned, a really awful smile that looked like it might split his face. "You really are. Alright, a gift, a gift for the fairy queen, what the fuck could she possibly want?" he mused.

It took the Devil maybe five minutes to come up with something. He spun the gift out of nothing, his horrible spindly fingers dancing through the air until he set the gift down on the table. June stared at it, mesmerized by what his king had created.

Lucifer studied his creation briefly. "And, you know, Junius...if things go sideways, let me know, won't you?"

"Thank you."

"I won't pretend that I can fix it, but I might be able to make things better."

June nodded.

Lucifer put one of his long, spidery hands against June's cheek, cradling his face and setting all kinds of feelings aching. It wasn't fair.

"No, but we've managed, haven't we?" Lucifer reminded, pulling June out of his sulk.

June hadn't meant to let any of that slip through.

Lucifer swooped down and gave him a hug. "Next time you better kneel for me, though, you know how much I like it," he teased.

June managed to give him a watery smile.

The Devil tightened his embrace and then he was gone, just as soon as he'd come.

MARCH 30, 1954.

A bad mood hung over all of them as they made their way to Central Park. Marie hated going to the Otherworld and June was impressed that she'd even offered to bring them there in the first place. James Kelly was on the verge of a nervous collapse because June had lost his temper and shouted at him. June had a combination of guilt, irritation, and fear roiling in his gut.

He had the gift from his king cradled in his arms. It would go over well, he thought. He hoped.

It was the middle of the night and they were sneaking around behind the Met, trying to interpret the instructions Marie's father had given them about how to get into the Otherworld. As they crept, Marie growled under her breath about how fairies always had to go and change things that didn't need changing.

When Maeve had lived in Manhattan, her court had been accessed by rowing out into Harlem Meer, throwing down a handful of pennies (or whatever coin had been on hand), and asking nicely.

Since her court had left, the remaining fairies had moved the entrance; it was a smaller troop of ancient Fair Folk who had little interest in humans. These folk would grant passage into the Otherworld, but it would be up to Marie to safely bring the three of them from the entrance to Maeve's court.

"A stone's throw from the king," Marie told them. "So, you know, keep an eye out for a king."

"Does Cleopatra count?" June asked, staring at where Cleopatra's Needle loomed against the sky. "Didn't she ask to be called pharaoh?"

"That was Hatshepsut," Marie said.

"I think it was both," James Kelly whispered, the first thing he'd said since June had shouted for him to keep his goddamn hands to himself on the walk over.

Marie squinted up at the obelisk and sighed.

Before she could trudge over, the vampire suggested, "There's that statue, though, the one the put up for the World's Fair. That fellow on the horse. I'm sure he's a king. It's not a riddle, is it?"

Marie shook her head. "I don't think so. Alfie always was straightforward. For a fairy."

They set off towards the statue, but once they'd gotten there, they looked around in all directions.

"How far is a stone's throw?" June asked.

"I don't know," she admitted.

"And, uh, in which direction? I mean, we aren't meant to go into the pond, are we? They've done that before."

"I don't know."

He opened his mouth.

"June, if you ask me another question, I'm going home," she warned before he could get half a word out.

He closed his mouth, scuffed the toe of his boot against the ground, and glanced at James Kelly. The vampire had his gaze fixed on the statue, his face scrunched up with his eyes slit and his mouth turned down at the corners. Every so often, his gaze would drift towards June, but he dragged it back with clear effort.

He was trying to puzzle this out, too, June realized. "You—"

"It's so hard to *think* like this!" the vampire grumbled.

June stopped, adjusting his grip on the gift as he watched James Kelly.

"What if...?" James Kelly rubbed his face and let out a frustrated moan. He kicked the foot of the statue. "What if it's...not an expression! A, uh...*Shit*, fuck. Literal! What if it's literal?"

June frowned. "You mean..."

"You know, *literal*, like you literally—"

"Literally throw a stone!" Marie cried, her voice ringing through the park. She found a rock.

"I mean, I don't, I don't know how it's going to tell us where to throw it but..." James Kelly trailed off.

Marie hurled the rock and June didn't know how she'd determined the direction in which to throw it.

The rock thumped against the ground and the grass shifted around it, scuttling away like it was made of spiders.

Marie grabbed June by the arm and yanked him towards the scurrying grass. All his instincts said to stay away from anything that moved like that, but instead of fleeing, he called for James Kelly to come along.

The grass cleared a space then started to move upwards, twisting and weaving until a doorway had formed. No door appeared and when June peered through it, all he saw was more of Central Park.

"Hold on to him," Marie advised, linking her arm with June's.

He offered his elbow to James Kelly, who wrapped both of his arms around June's, holding on so tight he made the leather creak.

Marie pulled them into the Otherworld, her face sterner than June had ever seen it.

Passing through the doorway didn't have the crawling-bugs feeling that it did when he traveled with his king; instead, it felt like sliding through a Jell-O mold and not just regular Jell-O but one of those nauseating concoctions with bits of ham and pickles studded throughout.

He fully expected to be slimy when he emerged on the other side. He passed through with a squelch, ruffled but not coated with any kind of goo or gunk.

Crouched on a rock and presumably waiting for them was a small fairy man, not a person in miniature, but simply willowy and short-statured.

"Alfie," Maire greeted him, not particularly looking in his direction.

His return was considerably warmer and came with a fond smile. "Marie." The man stood, revealing himself to be only a hair taller than Marie and not any wider. He was a darker shade of purple than she was, more violet than lavender.

The fairy's eyes slid towards June and lingered on the gift in his arms, neatly packaged and wrapped. He turned his gaze back to his daughter.

"Hold this," June requested, pressing Maeve's box into James Kelly's arms. Once he'd handed it off, he reached into his jacket pocket to draw out another box and offered it to Marie's father. "Uh. This is for you. For helping out."

"I hardly did anything," Alfie said and it didn't feel like false humility. "And when a daughter asks..." He spread his hands and graced Marie with an affectionate look.

June glanced towards the box, still holding it out towards the fairy.

Alfie came down from the rock and took it from June's palm, his movements as gentle as if he were picking up a caterpillar or something else he ran the risk of harming. "What is it?"

"Dirt."

Alfie tilted his head to the side, his narrow, upturned eyes flicking over June's face. His face was all angles, sharp and delicate. June thought that it was a crying shame that things had gone so sour between fairies and the fallen angels.

"It's good dirt, I mean. The best I can make. You've got to mix it with a little water. It'll grow anything, even things that are finicky."

Alfie appeared genuinely touched. "Thank you..."

June gave his full name, which was considerably more than he would have done with any other fairy, but Alfie had done him a good turn. "Junius Thompson, malak ha'satan, among the first fallen."

"Thank you, Junius Thompson, malak ha'satan, among the first fallen."

"You're welcome, Alfie."

The fairy gave him a warm smile, his gray eyes lingering on June's.

Violet and blue-gray, wouldn't that be something to see together, June thought, though the notion was nothing more than a passing curiosity.

James Kelly put his hand on June's shoulder, his fingers tightening, not painful but definitely edging towards jealous. June put his hand over James Kelly's and leaned his cheek against it, hoping the contact would reassure the vampire.

"Would you like me to accompany you to the court?" Alfie offered.

June didn't know if it would be the right move. If it would be rude to refuse or if it would be a burden on Alfie if he accepted. If James Kelly would be resentful. He settled on saying, "I don't want to be a bother."

"I wouldn't have offered if it would be a bother. I admit I am interested in how this plays out. I was rather a rapscallion in my youth and I can't say I don't feel a little guilty."

"I'd appreciate it if you don't mind."

"It's this way. A little bit of a walk." Alfie gestured for them to follow and proceeded away from the doorway.

His movements had a slow, dreamy quality to them, like a lazy river or a single leaf rolling along in a breeze.

They walked two by two, Marie and her father in the front. James Kelly walked close to June and sometimes he would make like he was going to take his hand, but he pulled back each time.

"I didn't mean to shout at you before like that," June told him.

"I wasn't listening."

"I always give you a hard time for being careful and now, I don't know." June sighed. "I don't know about anything."

"I'm sorry."

June put an arm around his shoulder, pulled him in close. "I've been arrested plenty of times, you know. Vice raids and all that. But somehow it still hasn't sunk in. That impulse to hide, I just haven't got it. Maybe I'm stupid."

"I don't think so."

June didn't want to talk about that anymore. He looked around the path; it wasn't paved, not exactly, nor was it dirt. Hard-packed gravel made of glittering white stone, bordered by large gray ones. Outside the path, trees climbed up towards the sky, which had purple tinge it didn't have on earth. The tree bark had silver notes and the leaves weren't quite the right color. It was alien but beautiful and June felt that same urge to settle down come over him.

He wondered if James Kelly saw it, the beauty of this place; he wondered what it was like inside his head. If it was layers of consciousness, this wish suppressing his real self, or one large blur with bits of himself popping out here and there.

"It's a strange sort of loveliness," June commented.

"Like you."

June looked over at him, startled by the comparison and cautiously flattered.

"Almost. This place, it's different than you are, but there's nothing on earth like it. That's all I meant to say."

"Nothing on earth?"

"No, of course not. There's not a single person on earth like you," James Kelly said; it wasn't any of that dreamy fawning, either. "I mean, even the other creatures that are demons, too, you don't look anything alike. You don't even feel anything alike."

June vowed that if Maeve took their request favorably that he would spend about a month straight just listening to the other man talk. He didn't ever want to hear him fawning again. He wanted to kiss him and know that it was James Kelly kissing him back, not some nervous compulsion. He wanted to say, 'I love you' and be saying it to a man, not a wish.

He said, "I love you," now anyway and James Kelly gave him one of those smiles, over-eager. June hoped that whatever part of him was in there knew he meant it.

"I love you, too," the vampire said and nuzzled in close to him, his lips brushing against June's jaw.

They walked together, June's arm around James Kelly's shoulders and the vampire's arm around June's waist. James Kelly didn't offer him anything or ask if he was angry.

Alfie hadn't been lying when he'd said it was a long walk. More than an hour, more than three. The walk took four hours at least and June didn't dare to ask for a minute to sit. He didn't really want it. He wanted to get to the court and get this sorted. He'd have walked until his feet bled if it meant he could have James Kelly back the way he was supposed to be.

He hated to think of what would happen if Lucifer had to be the one trying to sort out James Kelly's head. Even when it came to rearranging elements in the minds of his own subjects, of creatures that the Devil himself had created, Lucifer wasn't good at it. "It's easier to put things in than take them out," Lucifer had told him and June understood how that was true. The difference between dropping a handful of sand into a bowl of pudding and trying to take the sand out without ruining the pudding.

There would probably always been sand in there and who knew how much pudding would get lost in the removal.

"What are you thinking about?" James Kelly asked.

"Pudding."

"What kind?"

"Brain."

"Brain pudding? What's that, like blood pudding?" James Kelly asked.

June snorted and gave him a squeeze. "I don't know."

"Are you feeling alright?"

"Yes," he lied. He was feeling just about ready to either crawl out of his skin or curl up into a ball.

Alfie turned back to them. "We should be coming up on the court soon."

June took the gift back from James Kelly. Nerves came over him. "What do you think, do I look alright? Do you think I should have worn a suit?"

"You look fine."

"I like the jacket," Alfie said.

June smiled and gave the vampire's hand a squeeze.

Courtiers made way for them as they headed towards a throne beneath an impossibly large oak tree. June could see Maeve seated there, her throne a delicately carved wonder made of pale wood, lighter than pine or ash. June wouldn't have been able to venture a guess as to its origin.

As they walked towards the center, Marie and Alfie stepped aside, too, melting into the crowd.

June knelt before Maeve and James Kelly imitated him, hanging back by more than a foot.

The queen greeted him, saying "June, I didn't think I'd be seeing you again so soon. Not until next year's festival, at least."

"I hope it isn't an unwelcome surprise."

"No, but I do wonder what your purpose is. Come closer."

He moved closer to the throne and extended the gift to her. "I come to beg, Your Majesty."

She took the box, pulling at the ribbon. From within she extracted a crown, intricately woven and made of crystal-clear glass. It mirrored the design of her throne and June thought that was a nice touch.

"I was told your crown is an heirloom and it must come from a proud heritage, surely, but perhaps you'd want something that is all your own," he said.

Her crown had been inherited, but he knew no love had been lost between her and her cousin.

She studied the glass crown for a long time, turning it here and there to see the various ways it caught the light. It sparked wonderfully in the sun, almost glowed.

"It is lovely." She returned it to the box and handed it to an attendant. Her fingers went to the crown she wore now. "A master craftsman must be responsible for such a pretty thing."

"I'll tell him you're pleased."

"What do you beg for, I wonder."

He glanced back towards James Kelly. "My friend—"

"Your friend?"

"My boyfriend," June corrected. "He...You had the kindness to grant him a wish."

"I recall." She looked past him at James Kelly. "He had wandered off the path. Not the safest of choices. You had warned him, hadn't you?"

"Lured off, I think might describe it better," June said.

One corner of Maeve's mouth curled up. "He caught the eye of a few of my courtiers. You know how the young ones like to play with things, especially pretty ones."

June chewed his lip and glanced back at James Kelly, who hadn't stood up yet. June had advised him not to say anything and to remain kneeling. "It did him a terrible turn, scared him, you know?"

"I recall."

"He'd been drinking, too, and, Your Majesty, I...he was upset and he'd been drinking."

"And you had been fighting, I remember that, too. It didn't seem fair that he was unkind to you. And over such a simple thing. What harm would it have done to him to grant you a single dance?"

"Couples fight."

She blinked at him and June didn't imagine she'd had any lovers that argued with her. He didn't think that anyone argued with her.

"Please, I came to beg," he said.

"To beg for what?"

"Can you take back the wish? He...he made it under duress and I'm begging you to reconsider granting it. You're the only who can undo it, Maeve, you've got to know that." June didn't like the whine that slipped into his voice, hated the hard lump in his throat.

"He wanted to make you happy. You take issue with that?"

"But it's *all* he wants. I don't...I don't want him to be like this."

"How do you want him to be?" she asked, her tone light and curious. She even leaned in a little, as though his answer might be riveting.

"I want him to be the way he is...the way he was before."

She leaned back. "Angry and frightened and cruel."

"*Himself*," June said.

"He would die for you like this. He'll do anything you like," she told him and didn't seem to understand that June had qualms with exactly that. "He was afraid and now he isn't. He was hesitant and now he's eager. He was cruel to you, June, and now he never can be."

Tears burned his eyes. "It's not *right*, doing that to him. He didn't know what he was asking for. He's from Brooklyn, for Christ's sake. He doesn't know the first thing about fairies or wishes or magic."

"Are you accusing me of something?"

"I want him back, I want him how he's supposed to be. Undo it."

"No."

He didn't think he'd heard her right at first and when the pronouncement sank in, he didn't know what to do. The feeling started in his stomach, a horrible emptiness, and it spread up to his heart and his fingers and his head, pushing out all his thoughts, his ability to think and breathe.

"Maybe a second chance is in order."

The words bounced off his ears like gibberish. He frowned and asked, "How do you mean?"

"You seem to think things should have gone differently, that his wish was born from drink and fear. I'll grant him a second chance," she said. "But there are rules. You cannot tell him what happened. You cannot leave the festival. He must give you the dance you desired so badly."

MARCH 19, 1954.

The full moon loomed above them; they were out so deep in the forest that the Milky Way cut a swath across the sky, illuminating the path through the trees. Anyone who wandered off that narrow dirt path ran the risk of falling right through reality, so June kept a guiding hand on James Kelly's shoulder.

They reached a clearing the size of a baseball field and June bumped into the vampire, who had stopped walking. Past him, June could see that the bonfire that climbed towards the sky and saw at least a dozen people with flutes and drums, their music winding into the forest. People were already dancing, the beat of the music quick but not frenzied.

"You can go on," June was supposed to say. He knew he was supposed to say it. Instead, he threw his arms around James Kelly, elated at the sight of his blessedly undazed face.

"What?"

"Nothing."

James Kelly stepped back a little, not entirely out of June's arms, his mouth turned down. It might have been June's fervor that put him off, or nerves about the festival, about being seen by so many people.

June swallowed, not sure what to do. The sight of the bonfire and dancers didn't make his heart race like it had the first time; it made his gut clench and go cold.

James Kelly wrinkled his nose at June and took half a step towards the clearing. He glanced back over his shoulder towards June, who hadn't moved. "Are you alright?"

"Yes, sorry. Yes." June followed him, jumpy, nervous like he hadn't been the first time. "It's, uh, there really are a lot of people here, huh? And it's *loud*, isn't it?"

"Isn't it supposed to be?"

"No, it is, of course it is, I guess I just never noticed, you know. How loud it is. How many people." June glanced around, thought he spotted Kaveon's peach-colored curls among the dancers and ripped his eyes away. "Come on, let's walk around. I bet. Uh. I don't know. What do you think, do you want a drink or something?"

"Are you sure you're alright?"

"Yes. I am. I just. Would you mind if I held your hand?"

"Uh." James Kelly looked around, shoulders tense.

"It's just." June couldn't tell him, that had been one of the rules, but June was terrified that this might be the last time he'd ever see the real James Kelly again, the one who wasn't under the sway of a fairy magic, whose best bet wasn't getting his mind picked apart by the Devil. "You know how you said sometimes you felt like you might turn inside out?"

The other man nodded.

"Can I just hold your hand?" He looked around at all the people, all the wild dancers swaying together, and felt absolutely lost.

James Kelly gave him a pat on the shoulder and rubbed his arm, reassuring but concerned. "Are you sure you want to be here?"

"Yes," June answered, too eager, but worried what would happen if they left the clearing. Would Maeve bring them back right away if they broke a rule, or leave the rest of the night to play out? He led James Kelly deeper into the clearing. "Let's, uh, maybe let's get a drink? Do you want a drink?"

"I guesso, sure."

The music swelled around them, heady and warm, but now

instead of luring him, it filled June up with dread.

He found them drinks, wanting it mostly so he would have something to do, something to hold. Halfway through guzzling his, when James Kelly had only taken a sip of his, June remembered that being drunk had been half their problem in the first place.

He finished the drink anyway and kept moving, circling around the bonfire, as if moving would help. He'd read somewhere that sharks couldn't stop swimming or they would die and that was what he felt like, the world's most nervous, dread-filled shark.

James Kelly nodded toward the pine bough dais. "Those aren't more of your sort, are they?"

"What?"

"They're not really people colored."

It took June a moment to process what he meant.

"Human colored," the vampire amended.

"Fairies."

"Like Marie?"

"Yes."

"Oh."

Maeve caught June's eye and smiled at him; he knew he had to go over or risk her displeasure. He approached the dais, chewing his nails, gnawing, really.

"Your hands have got to be so dirty," the vampire scolded.

June shoved his hands into his pockets.

Maeve's smile grew as he approached. "Something told me you'd be here." She opened her arms for a hug and he gave it to her, almost flinching at the feel of her skin.

He jerked back as quick as he could and couldn't think of anything to say.

"I think I owe you an apology."

"Uh. No."

Her eyes narrowed a little.

"Sorry," he said.

"Sorry? I'm not sure that I follow."

"Uh. I don't know." June glanced around.

"Are you enjoying yourself?"

"It's loud."

She tilted her head. "I lent the band some of the best players from my court."

"Oh. Well. They're probably good, just, you know, it's a little loud. Don't you think it's loud?"

"It's a festival," she pointed out. "It would be unusual to have quiet music at a festival with so many people in attendance."

"Suppose so." He rubbed the back of his neck, kicked a stray twig jutting up from the dais. It snapped off and he looked at her, his eyes feeling like they'd pop out of his face. "I'm sorry."

James Kelly put a hand on his back and leaned in close to him, close enough that June could feel his breath on his ear. He whispered, "Do you want to keep walking?"

He made eye contact, gave a small nod.

The vampire pulled back, flashed a handsome smile at the fairy queen, and told her, "I just saw someone that June's promised to introduce me to. I hope you don't mind if we go catch him before he disappears again."

"Not at all."

"It was wonderful to meet you," he said. He put his hand on June's elbow and steered him away.

When James Kelly approached Kaveon, who was plucking a cup from the drink table, June stared, then realized his mouth was hanging open.

"He's the only one I recognized," James Kelly confided as they walked.

Kaveon spotted them and beamed, his face lighting up. "Junie! Hi! You know, I just had this feeling that I would see you here."

"It's a fertility festival," June pointed out shortly.

Kaveon's smile didn't waver. He took June by the hand. "Come dance." He turned to James Kelly and put a hand on his arm, sliding in close to him and giving him a sly look. "You too. You must be the vampire I've heard so much about, everyone was *talking* about June's new catch. They're right, you're very handsome."

James Kelly balked a little, stepping away from his touch.

"No, thanks," June said, almost snapping at Kaveon.

The other demon let go of June's hand and adjusted his proximity to James Kelly. He dropped all his slyness, all the slink going out of his body language. He had always been good about knowing when people were uncomfortable. To the vampire, Kaveon said, "Never mind dancing. Tell me about how this one has been."

Suddenly, June's sour attitude towards Kaveon felt wrong. He hadn't done anything to them, none of this was his fault.

James Kelly said nothing.

"You are the boyfriend, aren't you?" Kaveon asked. "Tell me I haven't put my foot in my mouth."

June opened his mouth, ready to brush off the question and tell Kaveon to mind his own business.

"I am," the vampire answered.

Kaveon handed them both drinks. "Let's talk somewhere, I want to hear all about how you met. I mean, there's gossip of course, but I'd rather have it from the source. I'm Kaveon, by the way, I don't know if we've ever been formally introduced. James, right?"

"James Kelly. What do you mean gossip?" James Kelly asked.

"Sure. Davia was telling me *all* about it."

"Davia. She's the one in Brooklyn, right?"

"She is. He hasn't introduced you?" Kaveon sounded scandalized but June knew it was fake.

"No."

"Oh, darling, you'll get a kick out of seeing Junie with the rest of them."

June wanted to smack him.

"How do you mean?" James Kelly asked.

"You know. There's angels and then there's *angels*. I mean, none of us are angels anymore..." Kaveon trailed off with a shrug.

"And which one are you two?"

"The fun kind," Kaveon laughed. "Right, June?"

June didn't feel fun. He felt miserable. He wanted to wind his arms around James Kelly and weep, especially when James Kelly gave him a small, warm smile.

Kaveon brought them over to the edge of the clearing and seated himself on the grass; from here, they had a good view of the bonfire but were far enough away that they could talk without shouting.

Away from the roar of the fire, the night air had a sharp chill. June shrugged deeper into his jacket.

"God, look at them go!" Kaveon cooed at the dancers. He asked James Kelly, "You don't like to dance?"

"I haven't got anything against dancing," the vampire replied.

"Then why are we sitting here?"

"I...I don't know. That's not the kind of dancing I'd be any good at."

"I bet you'd do great."

James Kelly shook his head. "I'd rather not."

"Suit yourself."

How well James Kelly tolerated Kaveon's questions surprised June; even though the vampire sometimes blushed or balked, and definitely squirmed at a few points, he stayed amiable. Not a single mean look or cruel comment.

When James Kelly finished his drink, Kaveon offered to go get him another one and he accepted.

June watched Kaveon go. In a hundred years, he never would have guessed this would be how his last night with James Kelly would be. He'd refused to even think about having a last night with him.

"What if we only had one more night together?" June asked. He couldn't help himself.

"What are you talking about?"

"Just. You know. Hypothetically. If we had one night and that was it."

"I guess I would make the most of it."

It wasn't the answer June had wanted. He wanted some clever way to fix things. "Do you want to be here?"

"Well, to be honest, no, it's not really my scene. But you want to be here, don't you? I don't mind tagging along."

June chewed his lip. They could stay here all night and he could keep the truth from James Kelly, but there was no way to get him to dance. Nothing short of coercion or physical force would do it, as far as June could tell. "Would you mind if I held your hand? I know you're not keen on that, that you don't want people to know about us."

"You can't think that's how I feel."

"Isn't it?"

"No," he protested, like June had really offended him. "Or it's not how I want to feel. I don't *want* to worry, I just can't help it. You know?"

"Sure."

"It's easier when it's just us." He gave an embarrassed smile. "Or when I've been drinking."

June snorted. "Isn't it always like that? Kissing strangers at house parties? Do you want to get a drink?"

"Uh." His eyes danced back towards the bonfire, the revelers. "It's a lot of people."

"I'll stick with you."

"I'm not looking to get lit or anything but maybe a few more drinks," the vampire conceded.

Kaveon brought them back another round; they took turns bringing back drinks, getting a little bit silly. James Kelly sat a little bit closer to June each time he came back and he started doling out revealing answers to Kaveon's questions.

"What do you mean, the first time?" Kaveon demanded.

"I didn't say *first time*, I said *first time in a while*," James Kelly corrected.

June stopped looking at the stars, wondering what Kaveon was squawking about.

"But, I mean, how long is a while?" the demon pressed.

"I don't know."

"Months?"

James Kelly shook his head.

"Years?"

The vampire nodded.

"A handsome fellow like you? Going *years* without?"

"Not without anything at all!" the vampire protested. "Just, you know, some girls don't like to do that. I didn't have a lot of girlfriends, and besides, they were nice girls, they didn't do that kind of thing. Annie *hated* it."

He had to be drunk if this was what Kaveon had gotten him to talk about. He put one arm around James Kelly's shoulder, letting it dangle across his chest, and the other man leaned against him, nestling his face against the crook of June's arm.

"You don't think I'm a nice girl, James Kelly?" June asked.

"I like this jacket."

"Thanks. We can find you one," he offered.

"No, I like it on you."

June put his forehead against the side of James Kelly's head. "Stop talking to my ex about getting head."

The vampire tittered and hugged June's arm to his chest.

June tried to imagine him, young, with glasses, with his curls clipped short, asking a high school girlfriend for 'that kind of thing.' He wondered if he even would have had the nerve to ask outright.

"I need another drink," Kaveon declared. "Then you're going to tell me all about *everything*."

"Why don't you go dance?" June suggested, having been overcome with the urge to be alone with James Kelly. The festival would be over soon.

Kaveon raised an eyebrow.

"Go on, it's the last dance! I know you've been dying to."

"Don't go getting jealous, Junie," the demon chided.

James Kelly snorted. "Go on, give us some time alone."

"I see how it is," Kaveon sniffed, but gave them both a grin as he scampered away, plunging into the crowd of dancers.

"He must have been something," James Kelly said.

"Was he ever!"

"And...*he* broke up with *you*?"

"Why'd you go and say it like that?" June asked.

"No, nothing." James Kelly shrugged. "Just wondering."

"Wondering what?"

"No, I just...I can't imagine that he thought he'd do better than you."

June shook his head, drew James Kelly in tighter. "It wasn't about doing better. He just loved someone else. Better to go where your heart says, isn't it? Otherwise, you'd just be miserable, don't you think?"

"I figure you're right. We've got one stop left, right?"

June had to think hard to figure out what he was talking about. He'd entirely forgotten that this night had been part of a longer trip. "Sure."

He wondered if he'd have to make that drive home with him again, sick and addled and unyieldingly offering to do June favors.

"Unless you want to stop somewhere?" June offered.

"No. I just want to be home. You get to missing your own bed when you've been away too long."

"I know what you mean."

"You make this trip every year?" the vampire asked.

"Sure. Not always the same places. Sometimes I end up stopping over in New Jersey, too, if I've got enough people lined up."

"I'm sorry."

June chuckled. "Can I tell you something?"

"Sure."

"I love you."

"You tell me that all the time."

"Cause I want you to know." He gave the vampire's head an affectionate tousle, scrunching his fingers into his hair, kneading his scalp. James Kelly arched his back and leaned into the massage. "You know what you should do? You should stop doing your hair like this. Let it grow out a little more."

"I'd look like a bum."

"Don't say that. I can show you how to twist it or—"

"What do you know about my kind of hair?" James Kelly scoffed, burrowing further into June's arms.

"Lived on this earth of thousands of years, what makes you think you're the first man I've ever been with that's got your kind of hair?"

He ducked his head away, gracing June with a mean look.

"No, come on, don't be sore about it," June soothed. "I'd trade all of the other men I've been with in for you."

"No, you wouldn't."

June reconsidered what he'd said. "You're right. I wouldn't. I've loved other people. Really loved them, all the way down so it hurts. And I'm glad I did. Maybe what I meant to say was that I wouldn't trade you for any of them. That right now there's nothing I want in the world as much as I want to be yours."

James Kelly rolled his eyes and sighed. June thought he saw a bit of a smirk, though that might have just been the shadows; it didn't seem to be a gesture of irritation but of capitulation. "Alright."

"Alright?" June asked.

"Yes, alright, you love me."

"Deeply."

James Kelly didn't look impressed.

"Abidingly. Nine letter word that means—"

"You give the clue first, not the word."

June gathered him up into his arms and James Kelly twisted to return the embrace.

"Last song," came a voice like chimes from their side.

They both looked over; neither of them had heard Maeve approach. She had a strange sort of smile on her face, somewhere between bittersweet and triumphant. She might have wanted to be wrong about James Kelly or she might have thought June a fool for preferring him this way.

The last song of the night was heady and raucous, one that was meant to send the festival out with a bang. They could see Kaveon twirling wildly, his hands trailing along the others as he moved among them, his face tipped up towards the moon.

James Kelly gave June a look, one that said, "Can you imagine *me* doing *that?*"

June couldn't imagine it. He could hardly believe that he'd even danced like that; it was the kind of thing that could only be done in the heat of the moment and always seemed alien upon reflection.

"That's alright," June said, not sure who he was talking to.

"How about I owe you a dance?" the vampire offered.

"It's a deal," June agreed.

Without warning, James Kelly slid close and gave June a kiss; his offer felt like a promise, a real one that the vampire had every intention to keep. It felt like *I'll buy it when I get paid* or *We can go on your birthday. I'll marry you when I come back from the war.*

"I thought you might be right about this," Maeve said.

June didn't look up at her, just closed his eyes and waited for this all to go away, to be returned to the other James Kelly. It would have felt wrong to say goodbye. It probably only would have confused the other man; it might have even upset him.

He waited, but nothing happened. He peeked up towards Maeve, who was staring down at them with a ghastly look on her face.

"The rules," she declared. "The third rule. He didn't dance with you."

James Kelly frowned. "June, what's going on?"

"He was supposed to dance with you," Maeve insisted, but something about that wasn't right.

The festival around them started to shudder, the whole world gave an unpleasant tilt and then the festival was gone.

They were nowhere, just the two of them and Maeve. It wasn't earth or the Otherworld or even the place between worlds, it was simply nowhere at all. Everything around them was a dank, flat gray.

James Kelly scrambled to his feet, away from Maeve, stumbling as he went, dragging June along with him.

June gripped the vampire's hand. They hadn't left the festival. He hadn't told James Kelly anything. "The third rule. He had to give me the dance that...that I so desired, that's what you said, wasn't it?"

"It was."

June saw a glimmer and seized it, crowing proudly, "He did!"

"He didn't dance."

"But he gave me the dance I wanted! That was it, wasn't it? I want a dance with him, the real him. Unwished. And he promised I could have it."

She stared him down and he thought for an instant that she would leave them here in this nowhere place.

"We made a deal, Maeve, he and I. Demons make deals," he reminded. "Please."

He understood the rage. She had given them a second chance and June hadn't even asked the vampire to dance. He had flouted her third rule and she shouldn't have been obligated to give him anything at all.

Except that demons could make deals. Except that James Kelly had gone ahead and found a way around her rule without even trying.

"Let me go home, Maeve," he urged gently.

"Do not ever think to set foot in my court again, Junius Thompson," she warned. "Never again will you have mercy from me."

He nodded and sank to one knee in front of her.

Then she was gone and he was alone in the woods.

The other revelers had gone, too, and in the center of the clearing was a great black spot that must have once been the bonfire.

June hurried back to his feet and looked around for James Kelly. He found him doubled over, his breathing shallow and his skin gone sallow.

"Hey, hey, what's wrong?"

"I feel..." He grasped on to June. He shook his head and sank to his knees. "I need a minute," he rasped.

June gave him a minute, sinking down to kneel with him. He cradled the vampire close, feeling uneasy and sort of sick as things he didn't remember happening wound their way into his head. Memories of a drive home they hadn't taken, of a stop at Howe Caverns they hadn't made, of a night they hadn't spent getting drunk on the roof of someone's apartment throwing beer bottles to shatter on the sidewalk, like a dream that he couldn't shake.

It was the trip they would have taken home, if what had just happened had been real.

Unless it was the trip they had taken, if the second festival had been the real one. If that was the case, then why did June remember everything else? The memories seemed to lie right on top of each other for those days, making one jumbled up mess.

"Are you alright?" June asked.

"What happened?"

"I don't even know anymore."

"Was all that...the way I was, June, was that *real*? Did I really act like that?" the vampire asked with no small amount of horror in his voice.

"I don't know. Maybe. I don't care. I don't care what was real, as long as you're back the way you're supposed to be."

James Kelly leaned against him.

"Tell me you're how you should be."

"That's up for debate, really; what are we supposed to be like?"

With a scowl, June said, "Shut up, you know what I meant. Tell me you're you again."

"I think so."

"Good. You've got to call your parents."

James Kelly sat up, staring incredulously at June. "What? June, what are you on about? That's what you've got to say to me after this? To call my parents?"

"They think I've brainwashed you into being my catamite. I'd rather they didn't."

"Now who's using big words," the vampire grumbled, pushing himself to his feet. "I don't imagine the car is still down there?" he asked, nodding towards the path that would take them out of the clearing and down the mountain.

"My money says no."

"Do you know how hard it's going to be for the two of us to hitchhike anywhere?"

June made himself stand and gave the vampire a good long look.

"What?"

"Nothing, it's just...it's definitely you. Prickly as ever," June said.

"Shut up."

"I'm glad to have you back."

"Shut up."

"*Ecstatic.*"

James Kelly trudged away.

June jogged to catch up with him. He caught him by the arm and pulled him back, wrapping his arms around him. There wasn't a word that June knew to neatly sum up how glad he was to have James Kelly returned to normal. He tried to take that feeling, the overwhelming essence of it all and put it into a kiss. He didn't know if he got his point across, but the vampire returned the kiss in kind.

APRIL 3, 1954

James Kelly had been retying his tie for about five minutes before June went over and straightened it out for him. He'd put on his nicest suit, at his mother's insistence, to go have dinner with Patty who'd recently come back from Chicago.

"You look great," June promised.

He sighed, turned away from June, and checked himself in the mirror again. "I never said thank you."

"For what?'

"For not leaving me like that!"

"You're always thanking me for doing things any decent person would do."

The vampire shrugged. "Still."

"You can't really think I would have rather had you like that."

"No, but..."

"But?" June asked.

"But you could have taken advantage."

"James Kelly," June said severely.

The other man turned away from the mirror but didn't quite meet June's eyes when he looked in his direction. "What?"

"If you ever thank me again for not raping you, I'll have you sectioned."

"Oh...I. It, it wasn't that bad!"

"You're going to be late," June reminded.

The vampire nodded and went to the closet for his jacket.

June watched him shrug it on and wondered how it would go. By all accounts, Patty might be a wonderful girl. Elizabeth had probably not dredged her up from the Hudson. June wondered if he would end up as an affair. Again. It wasn't a matter of whether he would tolerate being second to someone's wife, he knew he would. What he didn't know was if James Kelly would break things off altogether if he did end up settling down with a wife.

Maybe he would fall in love with her.

A vampire settling down with a wife and kids. He could always adopt, June supposed. He didn't know if dead men could father children.

"Hey."

June took himself out of his contemplations. "What?"

"Come with me," James Kelly said.

"What?"

"Come with me. Maybe my parents will get the picture then."

"What picture is that?" June asked, cautiously optimistic and disappointed in himself for daring to be hopeful.

"That it really is the two of us or nothing at all."

"Your parents think I've brainwashed you," June reminded. "I don't know if I'm exactly welcome at their place."

James Kelly snorted, but his face sobered after a moment. "Anyway, I'd like you to be there. It seems stupid now, but I really did think they might adjust to the idea. Of us. Of me being...well. You know. A queer."

June had never heard him apply the term to himself. He didn't have the same kind of lilting casualness that some people managed, but June had faith that he'd get there sooner or later. "Give it a little more time. Maybe it's not so easy to adjust for them."

"Maybe you're right."

"I don't know, really. I never had to do this. Do you think I should change?"

"No, not unless you've got something that will make you look like even more of a degenerate."

June chuckled and grabbed his coat. "You know I was trying to do my hair like that, with all the pomade, but the horns really get in the way!"

The vampire reached over and ran a finger over one of June's horns, then gently raked June's hair back from his forehead. "I like your hair like this. Messy. It suits you."

June followed him out the door, checking his body language so the world would suspect him less and wondering what Harold and Elizabeth would make of him accompanying their son. Wondering what the hell poor Patty from Chicago would think of it.

ABOUT THE AUTHOR

Dan is a writer and educator who has lived in or around Wolcott, Connecticut for their entire life. They received their BSED from CCSU in 2013 and has written their Master's thesis on representation of women in same-sex relationships in contemporary Spanish literature and cinema.

What Everyone Deserves
2017 Rainbow Awards Honorable Mention
"Although the story deal with some real 1950's issues – discrimination, homophobia, interracial couples and hate crimes – it did it in a way that perfectly suited the characters and the story." - Divine Magazine
In this 1950s period drama, Junius is a New York City fertility demon with a crush. Ever since falling from heaven he's been alone. Except for the mothers and children he watches over.

James Kelly Rosenburg, a black soldier with snowflakes in his hair, walks right into his life with a big problem. James Kelly, turned vampire during the war, is new to New York and its prohibition against vampire killing in city limits.

Junius offers to teach him to overcome his bloodthirsty instincts and live a proper Manhattan life. Their growing friendship leaves them both conflicted as they explore a city both welcoming and alienated by their kind.

That Doesn't Belong Here
"I liked the ... atmosphere that he created, alongside the paranormal creatures that roam the street. I liked that he wrote characters I could emotionally care for. If Ackerman writes another LGBT fiction, I will give it a try for sure." - Ami, The Blogger Girls
That Doesn't Belong Here begins when Levi and his friend Emily discover an impossible creature in an abandoned pick up. The thing is wounded, frightened and the two friends cannot leave him to the mercy of rubberneckers and tourists. This novel explores what it means to be a person, as the creature, Kato, begins to display not mere intelligence or friendliness but what can only be explained as humanity. The question of who we are allowed to love arises for Levi and Kato, as they are not just crossing the boundaries of gender or sexuality, but of species.

www.ingramcontent.com/pod-product-compliance
Lightning Source LLC
Chambersburg PA
CBHW070314190726
48291CB00013B/1286